W9-BUQ-401

Giv

ALSO BY BOSTON TERAN

God is a Bullet
Never Count Out the Dead
The Prince of Deadly Weapons
Trois Femmes
The Creed of Violence

BOSTON TERAN

Giv

The Story of a Dog
and America

This is a work of fiction. Names, characters, places, and incidents are the products of the author's imagination or are used fictiously. Any resemblence to actual people, living or dead, or to actual events or locales is entirely coincidental.

Copyright 2009 by Brutus Productions, Inc

All rights reserved under International and Pan American Copyright Conventions.

Library of Congress Control Number: 2009923033

ISBN: 978-1-56703-055-6

Grateful acknowledgement is made to the following for permissions to reprint previously published material:
Tomorrow Wendy words and music by Andrew Prieboy • Copyright © 1990 SONGS OF UNIVERSAL, INC. and BEFORE THE WAR MUSIC • All Rights Controlled and Administered by SONGS OF UNIVERSAL, INC. • New Orleans residents walk through chest deep floodwater after Katrina (05082908042) permission of AP/WIDE WORLD PHOTOS. • Kennedy photo taken at intersection of Main and Griffith in Dallas, Texas on November 22, 1963. • CMF-74039737 Camp Baharia, Irag. A corpsman with 1st Battalion. 6th Marine Regiment fires his M16A2 service rifle to acquire a battle sight zero, permission of Stocktrek Images/Getty Images.
All Rights Reserved. Used by Permission.

Published in the United States by High Top Publications LLC, Los Angeles, CA. and simultaneously in Canada by High Top Publications LLC

Interior design by Pauline Neuwirth, Neuwirth & Associates, Inc.

Printed in the United States of America

10 9 8 7 6 5 4 3 2 1

THIS BOOK IS DEDICATED TO:

The Hearts and Souls of . . .

Lacey (Mz.El) . . . B.J. . . . Freckles . . . Muffy . . . Beau . . . Ursa . . .
Cyrus . . . Nicki . . . Bruno . . . Spunky . . . Roxy (The Roxomania) . . .
Shaitana . . . Thunder . . . Chloe . . . Dogo . . . Pearl . . . Bear . . .
Mister . . . J.R. Puppyface . . . Suzie Q . . . Mister Old School (Himself)
. . . Baily . . . Patches . . . Fluery . . . Scamp . . . Asia . . . Mischa . . .
Truman . . . Scarlett O'Mare . . . Sheba . . .
Mr. Rhet Butler (Retro-Active) . . . Chrissy . . . Spenser . . .
Buddy . . . Mattie . . . Lily . . . Cognac . . . Budd . . . Lola . . .
Magic . . . Doc (Herself) . . . Gracie . . . Tomika . . . Molly . . .
Juliette . . . Petie . . . Monet . . . Greatdog . . . Rosie . . .

all those forgotten or forsaken . . .

and as always, the late, great, Brutarian (Brutieman)

Giv

Prologue

M Y NAME IS Dean Hickok, Sergeant, late of the U.S. Marines. I authored this work, though I did not create its people or their stories. These, you will come to find, I inherited.

The book and its people became known to me because I nearly ran down a dog one night on a back road during a Kentucky rainstorm.

The dog, it turned out, had been made to suffer and left to die in a crate. But his will to survive, his determination to overcome the many cruelties inflicted upon him, and the ultimate and unabated goodness that abided in him even afterward, are the actual reasons these pages bearing my name, exist at all.

I was profoundly wounded of heart and empty of purpose as I drove through the Kentucky darkness that night.

I had recently returned from Iraq, the lone survivor of my squad, when my headlights bore through a sweeping rain to find him there, stumbled and fallen.

Both of us being on that same road, on that night, and at that moment, was not an accidental happenstance but the poetry of fate. For, as much as I saved a dog's life, he saved mine. And he saved a little boy's life . . . but that is for later in the story.

I would like you to know, here and now, this story does not unfold in the traditional way. What it does, in essence, is follow a dog known as GIV on his journey across the America of 9/11 and Katrina and Iraq, the America of music and movies, crime and beauty, love and pathos, God and goodness, and the eternality of human redemption and healing. It is about the people Giv met along the way, the lives he touched, and the effect those lives had on him and each other.

It was partway through that journey Giv and I came upon each other and so was handed the simple miracle of existence. By trying to do one good deed, I would be blessed with the opportunity to tell the life stories of the people written about here and fulfill at least one lost dream, and to finally no longer be wounded of heart or empty of purpose.

—DEAN HICKOK

The Father

1

ST. PETER'S TRUCKSTOP

•

EE THE DOG. *He is old and scarred but still strong. He comes out of a desert dawn and makes his way through the burning heat of day. He follows the highway west through terrain that is barbarous and wild. A land as old as creation, and where specters of dust rise like anonymous djinns only to disappear again and again. Could these be his ancestors calling to him, guiding him toward a destiny that awaits?*

He trudges on toward the setting sun. He is alone. No one speaks his name, no one calls to him with love. He has no one to watch over, no one to watch over him. Poets have written about the dog; historians have told of his line. From Africa to Rome, from Egypt to Asia. There is nowhere man has been that dog was not there, too. Where one has left tracks, the other's footprints are beside them. He is part of the living consciousness, essential to our eternal conscience.

This is a great soul fallen on hard times. The worst was not the beatings, or the physical hunger. He has known both. The years of being made to fight in the dog pits and being turned into a violent beast were not the worst. Nor were the devastating hatreds exacted against him. It was being without love. To be nothing to anyone is to be nothing at all. That can leave the flesh bare and make living unbearable.

He knows that he does not have long to live. He can feel the whisper of wear and years working inside him. But he keeps on. Something drives him toward an unknown place that he senses exists. He can feel it all the way down in the thread of his blood. Somewhere he will come upon a sunrise where he can be childlike and pure again. Where he will be given a chance, a means, a way, a home, a friend, and the emptiness and wear will mean nothing. The strong light of beauty will outshine everything.

I watch his shadow move across the earth, and I know what others can only imagine. All shadows merge into one. From heaven to darkness—all are part of the same breath that created the world.

I see his tired face and the muzzle going grey, yet he retains the quiet determination that is blind and weightless to despair. He haunts the outer edges of a gas station or a motel looking for scraps of food. He drinks from puddles at the base of runny faucets in a rest stop. He has sores that have yet to heal and new ones that have just surfaced.

At night he follows the Dog Star during that time Sirius is closest to the earth. The headlights of trucks and cars pass with a ferocity that his kind never imagined. He feels the great wave of

*their power and his body shudders. At these moments he feels most
alone and vulnerable.*

*You've seen these silent migrants along the side of the roads,
searching through alleys of garbage, watching from behind junk-
yard fences or shelter cages. Even in their most deplorable and tragic
state they are still everything the creator meant in the creation, and
more. In that way they are so much like man, even down to one
moment of sublime defiance at that orchestrated beginning. Of that
other beginning, I will tell you later, when the tale is done.*

*Of all the books written through all the centuries by all the
poets and historians, there is nothing in the gospel of life on earth
that this old one is not a part of, for he carries in his blood the
ashes of his ancestors, who were there at the wondrous instant
known as the incomprehensible.*

ONE NIGHT ALONG the journey, it began to storm. It
started first as a bluish flash on the far horizon and the
earth came up momentarily out of the darkness. He was
making his way through hills that rose like sandstone cities
fashioned out of a howling wind. This was the country of
the first Basketmakers, the Anasazi, who had lived before
the land had been profoundly altered with such reckless
disregard. It was the country of the Conquistadors who
had come hunting for gold and with an iron will managed
only to fashion their own destruction. The road here was
all blackness, and soon there was another bluish flash followed by a rolling nocturne until overhead the sky quaked.

The earth again came up momentarily in a terracotta masterpiece of tested time that defied description.

The rain finally came, and when it did, it was at a hard, bleak angle, and as he made his way up a long incline the dog slung his head down to protect his eyes. He marched on like this for miles, growing ever more weary, desperate for a place to rest, to maybe find food. Nearing exhaustion he faced another rise and then another. Only on this last rise, he picked up a smell. He caught it momentarily on the changing wind.

Dogs. He could smell them. Not one, not two, not ten, but a whole world of them. These were not wolves, whom he had known and fought: these were dogs. They were just a faint rumor at first, but as the wind kept changing, the smell grew stronger and stronger.

He had lived long enough to learn from man that a road would take you somewhere. Roads always did. To a gas station, a coffee shop, some outpost of human life where there were trashcans and Dumpsters and sheds with overhanging roofs and crawlspaces beneath abandoned buildings where one could get out of the rain and be safe and dry, if only for a while.

But there was something more powerful and immediate on those traces of wind. In man you might describe it as the moment which comes upon you when you smell a perfume that recalls your mother or a time with family; it could be the pull of emotions from childhood that lie buried but not forgotten and which surface because of a favorite song or film. For others it might be that time after meditation or prayer when you feel calm and complete and connected and truly at the service of the universe.

Unlike man, a dog is all feeling. He is not endlessly mired in guesswork and probability. He never ends up being too smart by half. The man may well have held to a stay-the-course-philosophy and continued on the road; the dog did not.

He made his way through a shifting landscape, charting his course with a sextant of wind and a divining muzzle, until finally, descending a shaly escarpment, he came upon a terminus of light hovering there in the rain above yet another road.

It was a sign that radiated blue letters against a white-hot neon background. The sign read: ST. PETER'S TRUCKSTOP.

He came out of the din and put his nose to the wind and he knew—he had reached his destination.

THIS TRUCKSTOP, too, had fallen on hard times. There were still postcards of it in the motel office back when it was neat and clean; that was before the new highway with its faceless antiseptic franchises. The coffee shop had long since closed. There was a tiny gas station like you see in midnight, black-and-white movies, that fronted half a dozen bungalows. One bungalow is where the owner, Anna Perenna, lived.

This was not actually her name. She had changed it when

she immigrated to the United States after the Hungarian Revolution. On the night the dog arrived in 1995, Anna was forty-seven years old.

As a child, Anna had been orphaned when tanks with the Red Star came down the cobblestone streets of Budapest in long and violent columns. She had been in Pest when they opened fire on a demonstration near the Parliament. The soldiers had been lied to and told they were fighting in Panama, so there would be no chance of them showing mercy to a sister nation. Anna witnessed her parents being gunned down. She was trampled in the chaos that followed—an arm was broken. She watched as flamethrowers were put to the wounded and dying.

After that she'd fled across the river to Buda, to search for her family, only to learn an uncle had been murdered when a trolley was bombed. She'd heard a nephew had been trapped in a basement with other freedom fighters, that hoses were forced through the windows and floor, and so the freedom fighters had drowned.

Anna wandered the streets for days trying to find an aunt. Her arm hung at a bent angle. She ate garbage, drank gutter water. She came upon the corpses of children her own age in the cratered streets, their limbs torn off, faces hollowed out from weapons fired against their skulls. She learned in those days the poisonous tortures that man will inflict upon his fellow man.

She'd hid in the basement of a bakery for days with a small dog she'd found wandering in the street. She clung to it to try and relieve her fear; she trembled against it when tanks passed overhead and the building walls shook. She cried out at the dark and the want and the death of her parents as she cradled this small life in her arms.

But the dog's steady tenderness had done something else. It had aroused in her the need to protect and save it, and so, by extension, protect and save herself.

Would either have survived without the other? Would either have lived to later ride the ferry past the Statue of Liberty with an aunt of Anna's who had a tiny apartment by the Brooklyn trainyards?

ANNA BECAME A nurse and worked at the VA Hospital in Westwood, California. She met her husband, a wounded pilot, at the Wadsworth Theatre that was on the hospital grounds. They went to a small bar that night near the UCLA campus that was just below street level.

He had flown a Medivac chopper, and the war had left him deeply scarred. He was incapable of talking about the atrocities he had witnessed until he discovered what Anna had survived as a little girl.

They came through that dark course of history together. They were not above being shamelessly sentimental and were married to the Roberta Flack song "The First Time Ever I Saw Your Face." His mother had offered one simple wisdom, "*When you're having troubles, practice that it's spring and you've just met.*"

He bought her a dog for one birthday and a journal so she could begin a new diary. The dog came in a basket wearing a cardboard crown.

They took to the road as often as they could, trying to capture the innocence of youth that had eluded them. They slept in the sun and enjoyed the small things on earth. During that time there were no unwanted seasons, no shortage of small miracles.

Anna was driving. Husband and dog were asleep. It was like a secret place, in the car that night—a soothing tableau of an American family somewhere in the high pine forests of the nation. Then in the first arc of a turn, something dark and shapeless came out upon them from beyond a stand of trees.

The next moment, she was staring up at the heavens in the rain, the cold indifferent asphalt against her back. Then she was just falling away, like a meteorite through blind starless depths.

Anna alone survived. For three months she lay in a coma. When she came to, she was never the same again.

She had a severely fractured skull. The doctors were uncertain until after she regained consciousness what kind of brain damage she might have suffered. It turned out she had lost part of her hearing, and she had become light sensitive and would have to wear sunglasses from before dawn till after dusk for the rest of her life. But there was something else they didn't realize at first. Anna had become hyperosmic.

Her sense of smell had been heightened, magnified an endless number of times. She would lie there with ribbons of white light across her bed, eyes closed, and she would know all the nurses by their smell before they even entered her room. She could follow someone's scent up and down the corridors. She got to know her way around the hospital purely by smell. Perfumes, antiseptics—these were now pure sensory overload. It was overwhelming and decidedly disturbing. Everything was so intense. The doctor, almost joking, but with a vein of seriousness, said, "Now you have an idea what it must be like for a dog. Only they seem to enjoy it a lot more than you are."

When Anna left the hospital she packed a van with all her worldly possessions, the little money she had, and took to the road. Maybe wandering would stem the tide of grief. Months passed, miles passed, but she was half-absent from all of it. An emptiness was settling in that began to feel permanent, and Anna grew petrified.

Looking for a motel one night, exhausted and lost, she came upon a crown of light hovering above the road far ahead. It was a motel sign.

St. Peter's was run by an old woman then who looked to be the grandmother of time herself. She was prickly and smoked and got into your personal life immediately, as if opening a trunk in your attic and rummaging through it.

They sat in the office all that night and talked. The old woman could be funny and her speech was laced with blue language. She liked a shot of whiskey with her coffee and she drank a lot of coffee. Sometimes the road to dealing with our sorrows runs through a stranger, and Anna was in dire need of unburdening her soul.

It was getting on to dawn when the old woman said, "You know what you need, girl? You need a home. In here," and she leaned over and touched the young woman's heart.

Anna remained at St. Peter's. She was blessed to be given a mother for the one she'd lost. And the old woman, she was blessed to be given the daughter she never had.

But these were not the only blessings. There was another. One night Anna awoke to a smell that felt of animal, blood and fear.

She stood on her porch in that late hour trying to pinpoint the scent. She moved through the darkness and silence and made what little wind there was work for her. Up the road she went slowly, barefoot and in a t-shirt and nothing more.

A smallish dog not much more than a pup lay in the brush unconscious, its body wound around like a hoop. And that was how the next chapter of her lifepath began.

The nurse in her nurtured the dog back to health. And when it awoke and licked her hand and looked up at Anna with what she felt was expectation and trust, Anna experienced a perfect moment. Suddenly, there was an outpouring of the little girl in her, the one with all those unscathed dreams.

She gave the dog a home. Then she found another dog

starving and gave it a home. Once at the coffee shop in town she picked up a scent and discovered a dog out back behind the Dumpster. It had been badly beaten and abandoned and was well into a pregnancy. She gave that dog a home.

Word got around about this eccentric young woman who always wore sunglasses and collected dogs, never mind that she lived at St. Peter's with "the crazy old crone."

As Anna got to be known, she told people about her life, the accident, and about being hyperosmic. Of course, no one would believe her. So, to prove the point she had herself blindfolded once in the coffee shop, and as each local was paraded in front of her, she named them by their smell.

Eccentric is what they called Anna to her face. Behind her back they were much less kind. She was usually referred to as "the witch."

How many dogs lived out their time on earth at St. Peter's? Anna had begun a garden, as she had a way with all things living. What started as a small plot grew to well over an acre. She created wondrous walkways with places to sit and enjoy the smells and the silence. There was a gazebo, a picnic table. One could read there, take in the sun, meditate and pray, or be just plain lazy.

But there was something else about the garden. This was where each dog was buried when their time came. The headstones were made from natural boulders that Anna either carried or dragged to the site. She chiseled out each dog's name, and after a desert rain when the sun returned, the carved letters literally shined.

This is where the old woman, when it was her time to be given over to death, asked Anna to have her ashes buried. She even picked out the stone she wanted placed upon that spot, but asked Anna a favor. Have nothing written on that fired rock, except "mother."

THE OLD DOG who came upon St. Peter's on that rainy night had smelled on the wind those who had passed before him. They may have been beyond the years of leaving shadows on earth, but they were not beyond leaving the essence of their origins. The dog came off the escarpment through craggy scrub oak and down to the garden, moving among the resting places with their named headstones.

The dog awoke Anna, as so many had before it. She had picked up the scent in her sleep. She had been dreaming at the time. It was a dream she had lived through for years. Husband and dog calling out in desperation from the edges of sleep for the life they never had. She could not find them in the grey and windswept haze, for they were only ghosts.

Anna rose and went to the window. This night would have a profound effect on that dream, and the dream would have a profound effect on a life that was yet to be born. But it would take years before Anna understood that all her suffering had not been without purpose.

Living with Anna at St. Peter's was one dog named Angel. Angel, who was blind, sat huddled up beside Anna as she looked out the window. Angel let out a sigh-like sound to let Anna know something was close. Anna saw him in the storming darkness, nearly apparitional, standing beneath the St. Peter's sign that was reflected upon the waters he stood in, the blue and white neon glistening like a congress of stars.

2

G - I - V

SEE THE DOG. *Lashed by rain and measuring the woman who approaches. Without moving, he tests the air she carries with her. Streams of water drip from muzzle and face that are deeply scarred and must have been painfully so, and that may only be known by the one who carries the remainders of such inhuman mistreatment.*

They are there in the desert darkness dripping wet—the electric blue and white pearls of neon a nightscape of light they stand in deciding about each other.

Anna could see more clearly now the hard evidence of his life marked there on the flesh. It had not destroyed the dog's handsomeness. On the contrary, the scars were nothing more than scars. And this creation, even at his most threadbare, still dressed with pride and self-respect.

She put a hand out slowly, carefully, palm up. Would he

run, would he bare his teeth? He did neither. His head just angled slowly sideways and those eyes remained on her with mute patience.

She put out her other hand and in the palm was a bit of food. Water fell from her waiting fingers as he smelled the air and then took that first step and the puddle he stood in sloshed and that universe of neon across the surface rippled apart then rippled back and finally there was the wet of his muzzle against the cool soft of her palm.

As he ate, she offered, "You know what you need, old timer? You need a home."

This is how their time all together began. But the old dog did not come into Anna's bungalow that night even at her prompting. Rather, he went only so far as the porch and lay by the front door facing the world.

Anna watched him through the window from the perfect calm of the dark. His head rested on outstretched paws. The rain was the only constant in the wet, black loneliness. There was something about this dog, this moment, that brought up deep reservoirs of loss that passages of time could not resolve, but only limit. Maybe that's what she felt emanating from the weathered face sleeping in the quiet shadows by her front door.

THAT FIRST NIGHT Anna noticed the dog wore an unusual collar. What clue, she wondered, might it hold to his past? She did not bother about it that day, nor the next, but rather she let it settle in for the dog that this was his home.

The collar, though, intrigued her. It had been hand-sewn and was wide across the neck and made possibly from saddle leather or stropping leather. It would have been beautiful once, but now it was down to a pauper status. A scrimshaw of gashes and cuts. And there was this piece of metal riveted into the leather and fashioned like the case-front for a pocket watch. This was in no better shape than the collar itself, being scarred and dented.

Through the office window Anna would watch the dog going slowly about the day. And when it would sit on that garden hillside and look out upon an elegiac American landscape with his back arched like a readied bow, she envisioned the dogs of antiquity, as they marched with hunters and warriors through the wet and the heat and the cold of some untested wilderness. She could picture him with jawseams tight and a grave stare, the air dense with the smell of woodsmoke from long ago campfires.

Beyond stoic, the dog proved to be near gentle to a fault. War-tested and wary, without equal at being watchful, mindful without complaint. The victim, she felt, of hardened years, doing the best he could to find a place and fit in, but understanding his tenure anywhere could end without cause.

Whereas Angel slept on the bed with Anna, the old one would only spend a little time resting his head on Anna's chest while she stroked his face. His head moved to her softening breaths, and ultimately, as she began to doze off, he would rise up, leave the bed, and pass through where the light from the neon sign glittered on the blinds. He would then lie facing the front door, for Anna's bungalow was nothing more than a living room and kitchenette, with a bathroom so tiny, you could not turn around without bumping into yourself.

It was on one such night, when glittery streams of neon formed laminar bands of color across the bed where they lay, Anna started to undo the collar.

The dog's head came up sharply; he pulled away a bit. It made Anna feel the collar was more than just a collar, but something of him. She wondered, could it be all he has left of a life long since lost to him, and the losing of this the stealing of memories? Of course, Anna realized these musings were as much about her and her own life as they were the dog's.

Ultimately he relinquished. Whether it was meant as a gesture of acquiescence or affection, she could only guess.

The collar was even heavier than she'd expected once she had hold of it. The sound the leather made, as she turned it in the light seeping through the blinds, gave off a sense of intense physicality. There was nothing on the collar whatsoever, no identification of any kind to suggest where the dog had been or who he might have belonged with.

And then there was that curious piece of circling metal. Looking more closely she could see it had actually been riveted into a base plate inserted into the leather. She tapped it and found the covering made this slight echo, much like what you'd hear when a fingernail taps an empty jar.

Someone had put creative effort and care into this. What was the why of it? Was it some decorative embellishment, a moment of personal significance? She sat and flipped on the reading lamp beside her pullout bed. She crouched over the collar like some jewel expert studying a rare gem.

At first it was just a texture of scars and gashes furrowed with years of grit and rust. She wetted a bit of sheet with her tongue and tried to clean the covering. It did little, really. But as she angled the collar this way and that, she noticed, or thought she noticed, hidden behind the wear and deeply faded in the metal, the hint of what might be the jigsaw remains that could be letters.

⁓

BOB BORON WAS living in a padlocked storefront in a sleepy town not far from St. Peter's. Bob and his wife, Emma, had once sold watches and religious trinkets there. Now it was just home to the lonely widower.

The shopfront windows were shrouded shut with American flags. Anna could hear him inside, talking aloud dramatically. She rang the buzzer and it wasn't long before the talking ceased, and then a thick brow and squinty eye was peeking out a hole cut into one of the flag's stars.

"Haaaaa," he said. And then the locks began to open one by one as Bob murmured.

The door wobbled open, and there was Bob dressed as

usual in a crisp, clean shirt and tie just as he had for four decades as a shop owner. "If it isn't the Queen of Cynopolis," he said. He then waved her in with a hand holding an open book.

Bob was known to read aloud to himself hour after hour in his tiny storefront that was now his home and which housed what was left of his and his wife's worldly possessions.

His wife had always gotten pleasure out of hearing him read. It didn't matter from what—the classics, thrillers, the Bible, the works of the little known, the unknown or the notorious. It was just the proximity of being together and sharing a single experience in the name of love.

Bob was an elfish man who smoked incessantly, and the people who knew Bob treated him with quiet pity. His wife had died two years back after a long bout with stomach cancer. On the day she died Bob put their house up for sale and closed the shop for good. The center of his heaven had moved on without him, and he just existed now with his memories, in that foursquare shoebox on a side street just up from the bus station.

He put his book down and took the dangling cigarette from his mouth and asked Anna, "Did you come for a visit or do you need something repaired?"

She held up the dog collar.

BOB SAT AT the same work desk he had used for four decades, hunched over, scrutinizing that piece of decorative metal with his jeweler's glass.

"I wanted to be a teacher once," he said, "but I came to realize I was more comfortable around books and watches than I was with people. Except for Emma, of course."

He began to work the casefront with mild solvents to clear away the grit and rust, all the while analyzing how the fronting was riveted to the base.

He smoked as he went about his business. Smoke of any kind was nearly unbearable for Anna since she'd become hyperosmic. And smoke usually distorted or overrode other scents. But as she sat there, she could pick out traces of the dog on that collar.

Bob kept mumbling to himself as he worked, and Anna would ask, "What?" but he wouldn't answer. His world was only what he could see through the jeweler's glass.

Finally he came out with, "Do you know the difference between a book and a watch?"

"No," she said.

"A watch helps you to keep time, a book helps you to forget time."

Bob sat up and fingered his way through a work tray, talking to himself while he looked for another jeweler's glass, and when he found one he handed it to Anna and showed her how to put it on. He then took a needle-tipped awl, and he pointed out marks that were once upon a time letters. "See for yourself," he said.

It was a tiny, near-perfect world of total focus. "Could I have paper and something to write with?" she asked.

She drew out the shapes on a yellow legal pad, elusive

spider-leg marks, while Bob began to work the rivets loose that held in place the casefront.

Anna put the legal pad aside and watched Bob work the rivets loose. Even when he'd gotten them all clear, the casing wouldn't move. It had been in place so long it was nearly rusted to the base. With a deft hand he jimmied it carefully until it finally gave, and once they could see inside—

"What is that?" asked Anna.

It was some kind of folded up ticket with printed writing on it. Bob lifted it out. It showed the wear of years, and the writing on it was faded, and when he undid the ticket, it fell into two parts. He pieced them together.

"It's a pawn ticket," he said. "Look there."

Where the crease had been, there was the name of the place, or at least what was left of it:

> *Kings Pawn Sho*
> *St Loui*

BACK AT ST. PETER'S that night, Anna sat in the office with the old dog and Angel. She had taken the two pieces of that pawn ticket and placed them in protective plastic. They lay there on the counter next to the legal pad with the scrawl that was the record of the letters on the casefront.

Anna called St. Louis information, but there was no King's Pawn Shop. What was so important that someone should hide a pawn ticket in a dog's collar?

"There could be a whole world attached to that ticket," Bob had said.

She assumed she would never know. That it would be something from time to time to tease the imagination but nothing more.

She put it out of her mind and went back to that scrawl of letters. She and Bob were agreed that from the size and spacing, the original word was somewhere between seven and five letters. Of the three remaining shapes they were certain the middle letter was an *I.* The one to the left of it, either a *G* or a *C*. And the one to the right of the *I,* either a *V* or a *W.*

She laid out the letters in orderly combinations, and the closest she got to a word, or part of something that made sense to her as a word, was *G-I-V.*

It was time to close the office down for the night. She shut off the interior lights and sat there with the ripply glow of the St. Peter's sign reflecting off the glass. She was thinking. She'd call him GIV, as in the word give.

Then the phone rang. It was Bob Boron, the watch repairman. Right off he started talking away, "Today got me remembering. When I came back from having served in Korea, I was quite troubled. Emma thought a trip across the country would do me good. You know, see the world fresh, new. I had been a prisoner-of-war for nearly a year. Did Emma ever tell you that?"

"No, Bob."

"In my cell, I'd try to recall every book I'd ever read, telling the stories to myself, and what I couldn't remember, I'd make up. I did this to keep my mind from breaking.

"On the trip, we would take turns, Emma and I, reading to each other. That's how it all started, on that trip. We read *The Odyssey* and *The Search for the Holy Grail.* Emma saved my life on that trip. And today, that collar and dog, brought back memories, good memories. I want to thank you for today, Anna."

"You're welcome, Bob."

She put the phone down and sat quietly with that conversation. She imagined Bob and Emma in a car with the windows wide open and the wind blowing as they read to each other, driving through places rich and full with promise and where dreams could be shaped out of the sorrows of one's past.

She took the collar in her hand and glanced at the pawn ticket, then at the name she had written down and wondered. She leaned over the counter and with an unassuming voice said, "Giv."

3

GIV AND ANGEL

SEE THE DOG. *He has finally found a home after so much of a life being written in ashes. He gives love and finds love is given in return.*

The world of St. Peter's is one huge park with secret washes and ravines, water troughs and rabbit trails, shady porches and travelers passing through who pet you well. Even the lightning of summer nights is like a vine climbing to some enchanted point unknown.

Giv and Angel. Angel and Giv. Anna watched with curiosity from the office how Giv took to walking with Angel, staying on her flank a half step ahead. And she watched in amazement how with this simple repetition, Giv became Angel's own private guide dog. Soon they were moving in concert, their prints in the dust the unspoken measure of what it means to be one.

In the garden Anna had built, near the crest of the hill, was a yellow Palo Verde tree topping twenty feet. From St. Peter's bungalows, the tree seemed to cradle the sky with its nest of branches. This was the place Giv and Angel went to that was theirs and theirs alone. There they could escape the heat and wrestle their backs against the earth. There they lifted their muzzles to what the wind carried over the western mountains.

There was a photograph of Giv and Angel that Anna kept in a special place on the bulletin board by the pawn ticket. It had been taken by a young photographer staying at St. Peter's. In the photo, Giv and Angel were framed by the braided trunks and spiny green branches of the Palo Verde. They were stretched out with chests raised and heads high, while just behind them and encompassing all, the sun, immense and calderic in its descent. Two souls caught in an instant of eternity, at a place forever without a name, between what has been and what is yet to be.

Over time Anna would come to see other moments in that photo. A desert summer, for instance, when she was young and married. Then there was the watch repairman and his wife in their private world after the Korean War. It gave Anna pause. Was America just retracing old steps or were the wounded stubbornly and slowly making headway?

The photo would come to touch other moments and have other meanings. For one, it would be the last taken of Giv. For another, it would foretell the future, a future that was both profound and dramatic, and would ride down on them in a beat-up white van.

⟋

TWO BROTHERS WERE pushing it hard out of Bakersfield, California, in a heat so bad it was like having iron straps around their lungs.

The older was Jem, the younger Ian. They were nineteen and eighteen respectively. The brothers were hardcore rockers. Guitar American Dream wannabes weaned on Columbine and cable TV puke. They were trying to scrape it together till fame landed. They had produced a CD with money Jem had either conned or stolen. They'd gotten nowhere with it. "Some record exec is probably using the f——n' thing as a coaster," said Jem.

Jem's flesh was an endless world of tattoos, and one of them was a riff on an old Doors song he'd gotten from that S-O-B he called a father—"We want the world and we want it now."

Jem was the fire, Ian the soul. Jem had a need for the harsh and violent. His brother was easily overwhelmed. Jem was the top of the hourglass, Ian the bottom.

In Bakersfield they bottomed out trying to land club work. The white van they were driving had bald tires and an engine on the bum. They were drowning in credit card debt and cell phone bills, with not a sniff of action in sight.

Their plan was to hit Vegas for a couple of months and hook up with a stoner they knew there who thought he could get the brothers some session work, after that they'd swing on to Dallas. But for that they needed cash to feed the monster, which meant Jem had to go on one of his night prowls.

They'd been through Barstow before and Jem had put it on his potential score list. The Barstow train station was a pretty lifeless place late at night. Just a handful of the lonely, lost or waiting. So, Jem and Ian unloaded the van outside the station. The plan, as usual, was for Ian to stay behind somewhere with the equipment, on the chance that if one of these night runs went bad, they wouldn't lose the equipment. The equipment, after all, for them, was God.

Jem cruised a couple of neighborhoods with those manufactured homes that have been tex-coated to death and look like huge ugly boxes of cottage cheese.

He meant to find one with a little land around it. If it had a Suburban or a Denali in the driveway all the better. A boat or a Super RV was another sign. This was white trash, drive-it-and-wear-it, Club 700, armory-in-the-closet country. This was where people want to prove they put all that native ingenuity to work. And what better way than to hoard and collect? There would always be a credit card lying around or a checkbook. A high-powered rifle with a fancy scope, baseball cards, tacky jewelry. Sometimes there was even a little coke or weed tucked away in mommy's underwear drawer.

Jem had learned the art of stealing as a boy, from their father, of all people, while riding with the old man and Ian through rainy Seattle streets at night.

What to look for in a house. What to look for inside a house. Where to look. How to deal with security systems. How to deal with threats.

Threats were their father's specialty. Threats and dogs. They were both his pride and his poison, and his sons had the scars to prove it.

⁓

WHEN THE LEAVES of the Palo Verde began to drop, Angel went into season. On a sonogram, Anna could see seven tiny bundles floating in a black photographic sea. The time was coming to get the whelping box out of the shed behind her bungalow.

She watched Angel grow sluggish and thick, and Giv had to slow his walk for her to keep pace. Anna's bungalow was the original building at St. Peter's, so it had just a tiny fireplace.

She would sit in her nightwear on the floor before the fire, with Angel stretched across her lap. Giv would lie beside them and stare into the flames. She would ask, "What do you see, there in the fire, Giv," and he would slide along the floor toward her, that last foot or so, and get his head onto her leg with a look that was endlessly affectionate.

There are some dogs that touch you in ways you cannot explain. They seem to go to the primal forest and ancient well of the invisible beyond the visible within you. And once that place is touched, time seems to fall immensely around your heart for the months or years you're granted their presence. Giv was like that to her, as was Angel, maybe because their goodness had never been extinguished by the extreme cruelties exacted upon them.

⁓

THE LITTER WAS born well before sunrise on the birthday of the "Invincible Sun." With as many litters as had been born at St. Peter's, a delicious wonderment never ceased to fill Anna. Of the seven pups in the litter, a male died in the breach. Of the six remaining, five were female, the last born was a male.

Anna held in her hands this last trembling morsel with eyes shut tight. He was barely a shadow who couldn't hold more than a few spoonfuls of blood at best, but when you saw him you were looking at his father. You were seeing the elder statesman and old soldier.

As he grew the boy was forever following the father. They would climb the walkway Indian-file to the Palo Verde. The little one fighting to keep up but falling back and fumbling over headstones too large to jump. Giv would sit beneath the tree like some passive god, while the pup would snap and paw and climb about that body, trying to get a bite of ear or a bit of snout, all to no avail.

Then Giv would rise up and wrestle the little one down, and his floppy paws would wriggle wildly casting tiny spumes of dust upon the air. The father would take a leg in his mouth and just hold it there, teaching the child the order of their ways. Then he would lick the boy's muzzle,

and when their heads were like that together, Anna imagined the father breathing into his son the fires of his life,
the knowledge and wisdoms, and those arts of existence to
be passed on through him from the origins of time. Anna
imagined them wrapped in that same primal affection she
felt when she was sitting with Giv and Angel by the fire.

Father and Son would sleep side by side under the Palo
Verde as the sun moved, and as the sun moved, their shadows
would become one, and as it continued on they would sepa-
rate again, leaving a hard corridor of light between them.

⁓

GIV LAY BESIDE Anna as he had every night before he
went and slept by the door. But on this night something
was different. He remained close to her and Angel for a
long time, and Anna experienced from him a deep reser-
voir of emotion, a near clinging, in the way Giv pressed
into the spare stretch of bed between herself and Angel. It
was as if he were trying to close all distances, to become
inseparable from them, even if only temporarily. His nuz-
zles were so determined, so absolute, that she knew, as any
mother knows her children's most secret distresses, something was not right. Giv was trying to convey, communi-
cate, express what a dog cannot name because he cannot
speak. It is what we call love.

She held him as she never had before. She spoke to him,
she filled the air around him with baskets of praise. But
words can't touch the most simple affections. A kiss and

caress outlast civilizations, a soft hand can push aside centuries. And when we are about to die, a drop of love can fill the ocean of finality.

Giv then got up and stood by the door to let Anna know he wanted to go out. She left the door slightly ajar, as always, so he could come back in.

He made his way slowly up through the garden passing those who had passed on before him. He went and lay down beneath the Palo Verde ready to join the vanished, who go where the night goes and the day.

You are not alone, old one, for heaven is here in the great trees you lie beneath, and in the named rocks around you, and the earth that will cover your bones. Soon, you will receive thy bounty.

Giv had a tumor close to his heart that had pierced the sac around it. Blood was seeping across his organs. He lay with his head resting upon his paws.

You have lived long enough to see the circle close, to see your image and likeness sleeping by his mother in a tiny bungalow in the west. Because of you, through him, years from now, a life will be saved, and another after that. You will have passed goodness into the world. What better legacy than that?

So, close your eyes. The beauty of final sleep is that it comes without shadows, and before you even know, you are part of that vastness of song among the branches.

⁓

ANNA TOOK A flashlight and went out alone. She walked up into the garden. She found him where she expected.

She knelt and set the flashlight beside her. In its smoky arc she took Giv in her arms. She could feel the weeping come right up out of her chest, and it was as if her very bones were wounded.

Later, she found a stone from the blood-red mountains that had been struck in half. She carried it in a wheelbarrow to where he lay buried beneath the Palo Verde. As she chipped GIV into the rock she decided she would name the son after the father.

The Son

4

LADIES AND GENTLEMEN
—ANARCHY HAS ARRIVED

S EE THE YOUNG DOG. *He rests beside the blood red stone, paws outstretched, chest raised, head held high. And even with all the youthful energy that consumes Giv from time to time, when he is like he is now beneath the Palo Verde, focused from breath to bone on the far edges of the day, Anna can feel in him the stoic grace that was so much his father. It is, at times, unbearable and yet utterly beautiful and a treasure to bear.*

Yet, before they were even done with grieving, a white van rumbled into the St. Peter's lot kicking up gravel and dust. Painted on the side of the van was, LADIES AND GEN-TLEMEN—ANARCHY HAS ARRIVED.

Anna was in the office with Angel and young Giv as this beaten-up rig pulled to a stop outside the office. Anna noted another decal on the doors in I-dare-you-not-to-look-at-me colors: JEM EN I.

There was a heavily tattooed boy in the shotgun seat wielding a guitar. The driver was also a boy. He was the one who got out of the van and came up the office steps.

He walked into the office. Angel did not move, she just sat up. But young Giv, he went straight to the door and the kid——

"Whoa, man. Is it safe?"

The boy was genuinely scared even though Giv was just being a buoyant five-month-old.

Anna saw right away this one had no affinity for dogs. He was wary even as Giv sniffed at his funked-out jeans. It was the other one in the van who got out and sat on the porch and called Giv over.

Anna could pick up smells on people the moment they entered the office. It had become nearly a game with her. The tiny space seemed to encapsulate and intensify scents. Smoke, the residue of bar beer, grime, perfumes, fumigated air, unhealthy sweat, certain foods, even sex. What she was picking up from the boy who came in first, gave her pause. She handed him the registration card, "There's no smoking in the bungalow . . . and that includes pot."

The one filling out the registration card started putting on a what-are-talking-about stare while the other didn't even make eye contact. He just sat on the floor and kept playing with Giv.

"I know it's 'cause of how we look." The older one raised his tattooed arms as his defense. "My brother and I . . . we're musicians." He pointed to the van. "That's our band. Jem en

I . . . I'm Jem and my younger brother is I . . . for Ian. We're totally straight."

Even in the office, because of her sensitivity to light, Anna wore sunglasses. On this particular day the frames had these tiny, round lenses near the size of a shotgun barrel, and when she just stared Anna cut an imposing figure.

Jem handed her the card, "We're straight, man, I swear."

"Horses—t," thought Anna.

⁓

ANNA HAD GIVEN them a bungalow back from the road and set off by itself. This was where she put the ones who came to St. Peter's and had "potential problem" written all over them; that unit was perfectly triangulated to be watched from the office and her bungalow porch.

As they got into the van Jem glanced at his brother, "Talk about a freak."

"Let's just be cool around here, all right?"

"Yeah . . . we don't want the warden coming down on us." There was a little of the malicious in Jem's tone.

"You know what I mean, Jem."

"I know what you mean."

"And don't put this on me."

"I got to say one thing for her. She landed right on it. And did you check out those glasses? And that stare. She's like something straight out of a movie."

"She's probably got a piece under the counter."

The brothers were tripping it to Dallas after doing their

Vegas run. They had scored session work for some blue-pill band that played the lounges and who were working up a CD. They'd gotten enough other work from that to thicken up their wallets pretty well. But Vegas is the perfect pitstop for a couple of self-proclaimed sensations living on borrowed time. They ended up blowing out of Vegas after leaving a trail of outrageous parties, bad debts and broken promises. All of this was mostly on Jem; Ian's downfall was blackjack.

Now, some work needed to be done on the van, but St. Peter's had been picked because it was the perfect out-of-the-way place between two towns that Jem had spent the day initially scoping out, as he had in mind a night prowl.

While they were unloading their equipment into the bungalow, Ian began asking his brother in an edged-up way, "We're not gonna have trouble here, right?" He knew Jem, down into the heart of his dark spinning mind. If someone outdid him, outsmarted him, one-upped him, humbled, humiliated or handled him where it hurt his pride, Jem turned into their old man. Look out for the ghost, coming out of the cage, the one with gun in hand who told his two sons, "Cancel my subscription to the resurrection."

Ian said again, "Jem, I'm asking you."

"Take a tranq. Go for a walk. Have a cigarette . . . but disappear."

Ian ended up in the garden. Anna could see him from the office window, threading his way toward the crest, his shadow long behind him so it seemed from the way he walked he was pulling that long black mark of himself uphill.

He came to the Palo Verde and the stone from the blood red mountain with Giv's name on it. Anna was not ready yet for other people to be at the grave, and every time it happened, she felt as if the person was somehow trespassing on the tenderness that was her heart.

Anna went and sat on the couch to be with Angel and young Giv. He stretched across her lap. He was the only one left of the litter. Four of the females went to people whom Anna knew. The fifth went to an elderly couple who were now taking over the parenting of their granddaughter. The child had lost her mother and father in a small plane crash and was in dire need of extra affection.

The only price Anna expected for any dog was a picture of that dog with their new home and family. This was what lined the walls of the office. Over the couch there was even this beautifully framed collage, that was near four feet across and three feet high, of a vast number of the dogs that had been through St. Peter's and were now spread across the nation.

For the artist, the collage was a labor of love, and the centerpiece of the work, bordered by all these homegrown portraits, were lyrics from the Woody Guthrie anthem printed in rugged lettering which the artist had slightly altered to fit the theme:

From California to the New York Island
From the redwood forests, to the Gulf Stream waters
They share their souls with you and me

As for Giv, St. Peter's was to be his home. He would be the son Anna would build a future around.

⁓

IT WAS NEAR dark when Anna heard music. The brothers were playing. Their bungalow door was open, the lights on, the shades up. They were wraithlike cutouts with guitars, on opposing beds.

The one who Anna thought of as the hardcore, Jem, was the lead pony guitar, the down-and-dirty lightning rod. The other, Ian, Anna saw more as a counterpoint, the chaser, and yet there were moments from him of winged riffs that soared past his elder brother.

After it got dark, the van rumbled out of the St. Peter's lot. Ian was left on the porch playing by himself, and there was an empathy in the chords distinct and different from everything Anna had heard earlier. This brother had a more interesting and inventive vocabulary of sounds that spoke with liquid beauty. There was also a hint of sadness.

Anna was on her front porch with Angel having a beer when who should come wandering by? In the dark Ian got spooked by a sound traipsing up the gravel behind him. It was Giv, all spunk and interest.

The boy had his hands in his pockets and a cigarette hanging out of his mouth when he and Anna traded hellos.

"I heard you play before," she said. "Very good. I was moved."

He took the cigarette from his mouth, "Really? It's something I wrote . . . for me."

He seemed to her lonely and unsure of himself.

"Could I have a beer? I'll buy it from you."

"How old are you?"

"I got ID."

She pointed to a cooler on the porch. Watching him as he went, Anna corralled Giv with an arm.

Ian opened the beer, but then didn't just take it and go, as Anna expected. He looked about uncomfortably, and got off another drag on his cigarette. This boy was a billboard that said "adrift with no foreseeable destination."

"The dog is drinking your beer."

Anna looked down. Sure enough. Giv was heartily licking the foam across the top of her glass. She separated him from the brew. "He's limited to a shot a day. Till he's of age, of course."

The boy seemed to relax a little—maybe.

"That's a cemetery up there, right?"

"You could call it that. I prefer tribute garden."

She told him to sit if he wanted. "Where you from?" she asked.

"Seattle."

"Folks still there?"

"Our mother split years ago. FYI . . . she's a singer on those cruise ships. Celine Dion for weepy housewives and blue hairs."

"And your father, what does he do?"

Ian became this vessel of tension and memories. He could still see his father with the gun; he would forever see his father with the gun.

"See the dog," screamed their father, pointing at him with his 9mm. The shepherd lay on the living room floor bleeding to death.

Ian tried to kill the memory. He could not make eye contact except with Giv. "My father was a policeman. Then he went into private security." Ian did not mention his father supplemented his income with an occasional night prowl. "He also trained guard dogs."

"You must have been around a lot of animals growing up."

The smoke—Ian could still smell the smoke from the barrel of his father's 9mm poisoning the air. The shepherd tried to rise up. He tried to lift his muzzle to get a breath while Ian cowered behind the couch crying, calling out, "Morrison." Their father had Jem by the hair, "See the dog . . . *you* defy, *this* is what you get." Their father flung Jem aside, then he stood over Morrison and aimed the weapon.

The second shot killed Morrison instantly. The sound of the gun going off was near volcanic, but it could not overpower what came out of that dog's throat as he died.

Ian glanced at Anna, and trying to gather himself asked, "What's your dog's name?"

"Giv—G-I-V."

"Could I hold him a minute?"

Anna let go and Giv's curiosity carried him right over to the boy.

"My father was deep into music. Especially late sixties stuff." Ian left out the fact their father was a frustrated drummer turned full-time monster, who had to find ways to take his rage out on the world for being unsung. "He named all the dogs after rock stars. Mick Jagger . . . Janis Joplin . . . Jimi Hendrix . . . Jim Morrison."

Ian was petting Giv as he spoke, and then suddenly he just held him in a mix of the needy and protective. Anna watched. In those few moments, the boy was eighteen going on ten.

⁓

THE HOUSE JEM had staked out was a simple "kill," situated against a wash. No direct neighbors, with a built-in pool, formal gazebo, and brick barbecue.

The brothers were lying in their beds in the dark and Jem was explaining about the house and how the following night he might take a shot at it, when Ian said, "I was talking to that woman about dogs. She's alright. It got me thinking about Morrison."

Jem sat up all bitter and angry.

"I wonder," said Jem, "if she might sell me that young dog of hers."

Jem kicked Ian's bed. "We don't have enough scars." Jem pulled up his shirt to remind his brother about the wounds. "No more, no dogs."

"It wasn't Morrison."

Jem kicked Ian's bed again.

"He was defending us, Jem."

The next day was bad blood between brothers. And that night, when Jem rolled out of the lot, Ian remained at the bungalow playing his music. The pain coming off those chords carried all the way up through the garden where Anna walked. She, of course, had no idea he was trying to bleed out a run of terror in his life that included being forced to dump Morrison's blood-slathered body in a trashsite of foul lingerings and discolored shreds of matter. If there ever was fair and right, ever, Morrison deserved to be buried on a hillside like the one behind the bungalow with a rock of his own.

There was a knock at the door. Ian reluctantly answered. It was Anna, with a beer, and Giv, who made a wild dash for the bed and was up on it and down and back out into the night in an inspired flash that was pure roadrunner.

"I heard you playing," she said as he took the beer. "Did you write that, too?"

"Yes."

"A gift has been handed to you."

That was all Anna said. As she started away, Ian asked her, "Would you consider selling me your dog?"

⁓

THERE IS NOTHING like your faint steps, all hollow-sounding and strange, in the empty house you are about to rob.

It was quick and painless till Jem started through a bed-room bureau. A slender run of moonlight fell across a row of family photos. A member of the family, either a son or son-in-law, was in law enforcement. On the bureau was one of those institutional photos like he'd had to put up with at the home of his father. The proud guardian of established order, staring into the camera, the slightly angled pose, buttons neat. No primitive rapacity there . . . no! Just God, flag, family.

Jem lost it. This was no longer about just rolling the place. This was about leaving behind a touch of personal damnation, of dishing out some psychic damage for the years of it he'd had to down himself.

And Jem wasn't better the next day. A poison ran deep down into the hard prison created to hold all his anger. He told Ian instead of leaving that day, they would hang to the next. As a matter of fact, he'd already paid that "freak broad" at the office. When Ian asked why, Jem was secretive.

Jem had scoped out how Anna would leave St. Peter's for about an hour a day to run errands. The woman who cleaned the bungalows would watch the place and run the office. The dogs always stayed with her there. That would be the hour Jem would work Anna's bungalow.

Sometimes freaks like her had valuables tucked away. But this was just as much about violating her space, getting back at her for that comment about smoking pot.

A seven-year-old could get into Anna's bungalow. No doors or windows were locked. He peeked out through her curtains, could see Ian on their front porch tweaking his guitar. He had no idea.

Jem went through Anna's drawers, her personals. This woman was in dire need of something worth stealing. He went to the refrigerator and drank from an open milk carton just to leave his mark. He was about to go when he noticed an open journal on the dinette table.

Don't tell me . . . a diary. Ohhhh! Let's see what kind of stupid prattle she writes. Then Jem flashed on his name and Ian's. She was putting down her observations about them, and it wasn't prattle. She'd picked out certain fragments of their behavior and had the audacity to frame them with private observations. She compared the soft sad countenance of the one, to the cold steel of the other. All of that, Jem didn't give a damn about. For him everything ever written was just diary dreck. And she was a freak who ran a nothing motel in the middle of nowhere. People like her were born to be forgotten if they weren't forgotten already.

But when she wrote about their music, when Jem read that the real talent was Ian, that when she heard *him* playing *his* music, music *he* had written, well . . .

Jem understood about exacting pain.

As Jem stormed back into their room Ian asked, "Where have you—"

"You want the dog?"

"What?"

"We're outta here in five minutes. Then you run the van down the road, and wait."

[5]

STOLEN

*S*EE THE DOG . . .

When Anna returned, the woman who worked for her was running across the lot in a panic. One of the people staying at the motel had called and asked her to come to their bungalow 'cause there was a toilet that wouldn't stop running, and when she got back to the office, the door was open. Angel was there barking, but Giv was missing.

The woman said she had gone up the road and down, then walked the whole hillside searching. She swore she had not left the office door open.

An incommunicable panic came over Anna. Every bad thought imaginable, till it felt as if there was no room inside her chest for her heart.

She called to Giv. Her voice echoed back but nothing

more. The road was empty, and suddenly vast beyond belief. Her legs abandoned her; her stomach nauseated.

"Go back to the office," Anna yelled to the woman, "retrace your steps, check crawlspaces . . . everything."

Anna was already running toward her bungalow. She had a bullhorn there, and maybe Giv had chased a rabbit off into some prickly hole. Don't let him be missing or hurt. Don't let him be . . .

She wasn't in her bungalow a second before the scent of cigarettes and sweat as acidic as vinegar overpowered her. That smell didn't belong there, but she knew who it did belong to. She could follow it step-by-step. It was intense by her bureau and in the tiny kitchen, but around the dinette where her diary lay open it was absolutely nasty.

He'd been in her room. That ratty, little b———d.

She ran to the brother's bungalow to find it empty, their belongings gone. All that remained was the scent of cigarettes and sweat, acidic as vinegar. Vague fear gave way to something more virulent and devastating. They've stolen Giv. They've taken my boy.

You talk to the police. You can make out a report. But it's not as if you even have proof they stole the dog. What could be done? Anna slumped on the office couch in pure despair. Angel understood something was wrong and huddled close to Anna.

You say to yourself, make this be nothing more than a bad dream. Or at least a stupid mistake that can be rectified. You hope Giv will just come through the office door all excited and prancing

over some private adventure, totally unaware of the agony sur-
rounding his disappearance.

But as the day's shadow lengthens, you know better, and as
twilight comes, you wish you didn't. You cry till your throat feels
windswept and burnt, but you haven't even begun to cry.

Where is he? Where is my Giv? Does he know what has
happened to him? Is he frightened? Would they hurt him?
Would they cast him aside somewhere helpless?

IAN COULDN'T BELIEVE it had actually happened. The
van had been about a hundred yards from St. Peter's. Jem
was framed in the dusty sideview mirror sprinting from the
motel like a crazed thing with the dog hung up under one
arm, its head bobbing wildly.

Jem had leapt into the shotgun seat. "Take off!"

"What did you do?"

The van swung into the road kicking out flakes of brim-
stone and sand.

"You wanted the dog, I got you the dog."

"You just can't steal her dog like that."

Jem held up Giv by the body. The dog fought to get
loose, clawing at the tattooed arms. "FYI . . . I did."

"The woman never did anything to us. You're blowing
her up, man."

Just Ian hinting they should have consideration for her made
him want to crack "the talented one" across the face. Instead
he took Giv and flung him into the back. Just flung him.

The pup hit the van floor and tumbled right into an amp, head first. Something happened, because the dog cried out and the sound was pitched and painful to hear and it didn't stop.

Ian cursed at his brother then swung the steering wheel violently and the van skidded onto the shoulder where the ground just crackled beneath the tires. Ian climbed over the engine to get to the crying dog.

"What are you doing, Ian?"

"You hurt him."

Jem jumped into the driver's seat and took off, intentionally cutting the wheel quick to cause his brother to topple over.

The dog was confused and crying, and when Ian got hold of him he saw thin streams of blood trickling from the nostrils of that anguished face. "If you want to get violent go back and do the old man."

Jem gave his brother the finger.

Ian tried to settle Giv down and wipe away the blood so he could check what had happened. "We're giving him back."

Jem angled the rearview mirror so they could go eye to eye. "Not happening, brother."

"We'll see."

"Before we split St. Peter's I did a prowl of the freak's bungalow. See where this is going?"

Ian completely despaired.

"Yeah, that's what I thought," said Jem.

Of course, Jem had lied. Nothing had been taken. This

assertion was meant as a head shot to take out his brother's defiance.

The sun was burning through the back window and across the rearview mirror as they sped toward the Pyramids and Lordsburg. Ian leaned against the van wall and tried to caress Giv into a state of calm. The bleeding from his nose had slowed considerably, and the crying was now an occasional whimper. Ian glanced up at the rearview mirror where the light glistened. Beyond the glare, Jem's face was this unsettling ghost of the boy Ian had grown up with.

Ian had not felt so small and powerless since leaving home. He looked down at Giv. Giv tried to break free, to fight loose from this misfortune. There's no where to go, man, thought Ian. There's no way out of this great white faceless machine.

THE DESERT STOOD blueish in all directions from the Palo Verde, where Anna asked God to rain down on those boys bottomless misfortune. With teeth pressed against her lips to hold back the sobs, she prayed not only for Giv's safe return, but that the brothers' days be filled with pain and torment, their nights poisoned with despair. She wanted Old Testament justice in spades brought to the wicked.

Anna was in a complete state of wreckage as she sat by the elder Giv's headstone with Angel beside her, when the St. Peter's sign blinked on and the desert around the motel lit.

Even ultimate sorrow is not indifferent to what feels of the divine. That neon sign, like a photographic proof, brought back one of her purest satisfactions. It stood out as on that first night she'd seen it far down a beltway of road, when she was ruined with pain and anger.

She looked down at Angel with her milky and despoiled eyes that had been the product of violence exacted against her. She thought of Giv, the father, living beneath that stone and how he came to this place and found peace.

There is nothing more painful than to wish your villains well, nor fraught with more conflict than surrendering anger to compassion and forgiveness. To humble yourself before those who have harmed you demands that you bear goodness to the last drop of your being, even while your being is battered beyond recognition. You must take the pitiless objects of your hate and hand them pity, knowing full well they may hurt you, yet, even more.

There in the garden she had built, in the presence of those she'd loved and buried, and loved yet, she changed her plea. Beneath the imprint of the moon she asked, "Please, make goodness out of sorrowful men and sorrowful days. I know Giv will do the rest."

IAN WAS IN the back of the van lying on a sleeping bag he'd spread out. Giv lay off by himself on rumpled bedding made of dirty laundry.

Jem couldn't sleep, so he drove deep into the night. The inside of his head was burning with pride, desire, and fear. Too much selfish pride. Too many desires that had sent him out of control. And fear if what the freak had said in her diary were true. He wore earphones so he could power his brain through it all with some hardcore music while his brother slept.

Their old man had put the dogs on them. Sheer agony on command since the brothers were six and seven years old. He'd wrap them up in protective gear, a fake gun or knife in their mitted hands, and he'd set the dogs on them. That's how he'd trained the animals for attack. Of course, sometimes the old man was a little slipshod with the gear and had to stitch up the boys himself.

Jem and Ian had learned early about emotional assassination. That's what the old man had been doing. Training dog and boy at the same time. Training and breaking, breaking and training.

Jem looked back at his brother and then at Giv, and this sudden wave of gnawing shame came over him, and it felt like something had sunk in his throat. Jem was committing a little emotional assassination on his own and he knew it.

When Ian roused and sat up, a roadsign flashed past the rain-spattered windshield. A thin Texas drizzle. The drops coming tiny and fast right at the wipers. Ian came forward and sat up on the engine.

"I'm sorry," said Jem.

Ian glanced at his brother.

"About the dog," Jem said, "that was wrong. And what I did tossing him like that . . . bad."

Ian nodded reluctantly.

"Keep the dog. He'll be good for you. You like them. I don't know how you can, but you do. I'll be cool."

The country was a dark, flat plain and the few lights were like distant stars that had fallen to earth and were twinkling out their last. A sensation of overwhelming distance came over Ian, but he said nothing to his brother about it.

Coming up on dawn, they pulled roadside at a grits-and-gravy diner. Ian made a leash out of two frayed guitar straps to take Giv for a walk.

Giv had never been noosed and pulled, so he went into pure revolt. He just sat there in the Texas dust, unquestionably defiant as the gears of great trucks shifted past. Ian pulled again, but Giv refused again. Then Ian jerked that cable and stanched Giv's breath. The pup gagged, but he did not succumb.

The old man was there, leaning over Ian's shoulder in all his mortal glory explaining a dog is nothing more than a means to an end. *I am—that's what that damn dog is telling you, Ian. You understand. Right. Don't misinterpret it, Ian. He is teeth and obedience. Hunting dogs, field dogs, herding dogs, championship dogs, guard dogs, military dogs, even movie dogs. Stop their breathing with a leash and they will learn soon enough. You see, boy, you treat them like you would a child, or anyone else who needed to heel.*

Ian let his end of the leash go. Feeling no tension Giv

eventually stood and started to walk, sniffing at the ground. He tried to shake the lead from around his neck, tossing his head side to side, but it was to no avail. Ian let Giv walk on his own through a patch of weeds, but he followed closely, so if Giv took off Ian could get his boot down fast on the lead that hung off the dog's shoulder and snaked along the ground behind him.

THE VAN WAS hauling it through the hard, Texas heat. The air-conditioning didn't work, and the brothers were sweating badly. Ian had rigged up a dog bowl for water out of a supersize soft drink cup he'd cut down. When the brothers caught sight of the first road sign that said Dallas, they lit up. They had never been there before and it was high on their checklist of places. The Book Depository, the Grassy Knoll. Their mother had been an assassination freak. Name the book, she could recite you chapter and verse. She'd read a softback of *Libra* so many times, the book had come apart.

Once they passed that sign, as if on cue, Jem said, "What do we want to hear right now?"

Ian was up in a snap and in the back rifling through a bag of CDs till he found *Bloodletting*. He tossed the CD to his brother, scooped up Giv and jumped back into the shotgun seat.

There was a Concrete Blonde song the brothers made an essential wherever they had a live gig. Jem pumped up the volume and the brothers sang along, each playing out their part.

It is complete now,
Two wings of time are neatly tied

Ian had Giv in his lap and he got the dog's front paws up on the dash.

They say . . . good-bye
Tomorrow, Wendy, you're going to die

Then Ian lifted Giv's front legs and started working them as if he were the ultimate lead guitarist doing his sensation.

Underneath a chilly grey November sky
We can make believe that Kennedy is still alive.
We're shooting for the moon
And smiling Jack is driving by.
They say . . . good-bye.
Tomorrow, Wendy, you're going to die.

Jem did a mock wave at a passing bus like you see in all those assassination documentaries of the downed President just before the seams of the American dream were torn asunder.

I told the priest
Don't count on any Second Coming
God got his a— kicked
The first time he came down here slumming.

He had the balls to come
The gall to die and then forgive us
Though I don't wonder why
I wonder what he thought it would get us.

Giv could feel that furious rush of air coming through the open window and bent his way toward it. Next thing he had his front legs on the door then he leaned a little yet and put the other front leg out and up and got it anchored on the sideview mirror and there he was. Body halfway out into wild space, and the only thing keeping him from his death was the boy's hands on his chest.

There they were. And they rode like that with the wind and the fleeting earth and the windshield a burning strip of sun, with a girl singer leading them.

Then something came over Ian like a sudden thirst and he pulled the dog back into the van.

"What did you do that for?"

"Because it's dangerous."

But it wasn't that alone caused Ian to pull Giv back. Language is a poor thing indeed, if it is poured on dead roots. You can play a song a thousand times—hear it, learn it, live it—then one time, it's as real as salt and blood, and you are touched by the fiery design of its universe.

"Jem?"

The older brother was drumming the dash, "Yeah."

"We haven't done much with our lives, have we?"

Hearing that from his own brother was putrid. Jem

made nothing of it, no threats, no drama. He just killed the CD and drove, but there was that warring rider inside him working the serried edges of his rage.

Jem looked at Giv sitting on Ian's lap, totally at one with the road. He put out his hand to pretend he was trying to connect with the dog but Giv's head backed away, sealing Jem off.

Everything had been all right until they'd pulled into that motel.

6

THE GRASSY KNOLL

S EE THE DOG *from the sixth floor of the Texas Book Depository walking with Ian up the grassy knoll.*

Ian had wanted to see the museum, but it was pushing ninety and he wasn't about to leave Giv in the van. So, he'd sent his brother on, saying he'd go it another time. Jem was already fed up with that dog altering their lives.

Jem stood at the glass partition and looked into the sniper's perch. What had surprised him most was how everything was so small. The building, the perch, the distance for the shot, Dealey Plaza itself. He'd expected something larger, grander, more befitting a national tragedy. This was closer to a murder in a barroom or alley that you'd see on an episode of a television series. Purely small screen.

It was not the Twin Towers melting straight down into the earth and turning a skyline into smoke and human ash.

That was an event more befitting the death of a President. And yet, Jem could not pull himself from that seedy little corner where they had recreated the scene of the crime.

There was this primal and personalized electricity that poured through Jem. In part he was the charismatic leader, the rock star of the era, the fantasy most people would swap their lives for, the tragic icon of Zapruder Frame 232 with a beautiful babe in that so, so pink dress. Then there was the other part, the one told your talents are marginal, your relevance minimal—and you will never strike the right human chord.

GIV HAD LEARNED to walk with a leash. It had not been the most agreeable of processes, but it had come to pass over those first few days in Dallas in a back yard.

The brothers were staying with a sound engineer named Stoner they'd met at Nightland on Silver Lake Boulevard in Los Angeles. Stoner was near thirty and wanted to be a band manager, and the brothers interested him. He lived in Dallas just south of downtown and told them if they'd do the ride there he'd try and set them up with some local gigs. Stoner also had a recording studio set up in a guest-house that was decked out and where the brothers could record any new work.

Stoner lived in the front house with his father, who was besieged by Alzheimer's. Stoner had been caretaker since his brother, who was a guardsman, got sent to Iraq.

Stoner had turned the garage into living quarters of a sort. One large room, a bath, a wall air-conditioner for when Dallas weather got brutal. On one wall was a huge American flag and photos of Stoner's brother. In one photo, he stood before his tank somewhere in Iraq, shirt off, all dusty and sunburned. A top-end decal draped one shoulder. It was the movie pose of a boy not much older than the brothers that said, "I am invincible to misfortune."

Once the brothers were alone Jem pointed to the guardsman's photo. "Remember the other day when you said we hadn't done much with our lives."

Ian was organizing their equipment. Giv had already gotten first dibs on the sunken couch and sprawled across the armrest closest to the AC.

"I was just feeling—"

Jem pointed to the photo, "Maybe you should hook up with this character and chase some fool's dream."

Ian stopped organizing. He sat on the floor with his back against the couch, "You're not listening to me. Not hearing me—"

"You'd have free room and board. Free medical and dental."

"Can it, Jem."

"I've been doing my best to keep it together for us. Suddenly you're down on me."

"I think I'm just down on myself."

Ian took to rubbing Giv's head. Jem was pacing; Ian could see the anger and frustration start to kick in.

"The dog gets the best spot on the couch," said Jem.

"He's smarter than we are . . . and faster. Ain't you, Giv?"

Jem was throwing his brother an icy stare. "I think if you want to do something with your life, look for a nice war. Maybe you'll be lucky enough to be brought back home in a soup can that says red, white and stupid."

Ian stood. He took his guitar out of its case. "Stoner's brother, I'm sure, is trying to do something with his life . . . and I want to do something with mine." Ian called Giv. "I think me and Giv are gonna get away from all this poison."

IAN AND GIV made their way up the grassy knoll. Ian found a spot for them to sit in the shade where he could look out over Dealey Plaza and relive history. Giv sat a few feet away, as far as the leash would allow and just silently took in the comings and goings around him.

It appeared Giv had grown accustomed to his new life. He could be playful and affectionate, and he was smart— deadly smart. It seemed to Ian that Giv had forgiven them for what they'd done. Yes, it's true, they had power over him. The power of food, the power of the leash, of being able to deny, to order . . . if it were only that. But it was not.

A dog understands goodness and love. Dogs are looking for it in you. They are pure affection, a magnificent cre- ation of feelings, and a measureless dream that has brought life back to many an extinguished soul.

There were times Ian felt his life was broken water slipping through his fingers, and when this panic would set in, who would just suddenly be there? Giv—as if to lament alongside him if nothing else.

Then there were other times Ian was sure Giv understood that his real home was out there somewhere. Along with those who were part of that real home. And Ian was right.

Giv would suddenly become totally fixed, totally focused and strain against the leash. Ian could not figure it out. Was it a smell? A sound? Something seen? Could it be a moment that mirrored the past? Giv would not obey; he would not move. Then just as suddenly, it was over.

Is it possible, that which is sourceless in man, is substance to them? That they can pick up on prevailing mists that are part of the invisible world? It was at times like these, when Giv was locked into the faraway, that Ian thought of Seattle. And home.

He looked out over Dealey Plaza. It was quiet, only a small handful of people really. If you didn't know, you would never suspect that November 22, 1963 happened right there.

Ian's mother used to tell the boys that the tragedy was not just that a President had been lost. A father had been lost, a husband, a son, a friend, a neighbor. And what had made it not only a tragedy, but a never-ending and ultimate tragedy was that we had been connected then, one country indivisible in life as well as grief. And because we were no longer connected as people, that event would only grow in time as our ultimate tragedy. We had separated our life and our grief. We had become armed camps, so we could never truly embrace or console each other through the good times as well as the bad.

Sitting there on the grassy knoll and staring at a run of sun-bleached asphalt with a plaque pinpointing where the President had been torn asunder by gunshots, Ian realized for the first time, it was not just the Kennedy assassination his mother had been talking about, but a small plot of America known as their family.

The world just stopped. He was caught in plain view at that moment of realization until a voice said—

"WHAT A GREAT-looking dog."

Ian turned at the same moment that there was a sudden strain on the leash.

She was about his age, wielding a canvas carryall and wearing faded jeans and a so, so pink t-shirt cut off at the shoulders, that exposed some mighty fine artwork. And talk about a buoyant smile too good to resist.

Ian had only seen Giv this animated at St. Peter's. And when the girl squatted down and put out her arms, Giv could not get to them fast enough.

She was rubbing and scratching him, and said, "You know what I've got to do," she grabbed both sides of Giv's muzzle. "I just have to kiss you. I'm sorry, but I have to.

I saw you and I can't resist." She kissed both sides of his muzzle, and he licked her face wildly and she kissed him again and Giv's tail just took off like a windshield wiper gone absolutely freakin' mad.

The girl talked to Ian around Giv, whom she had corralled. "You guys are doing the tourist thing, right?"

Ian looked himself over, "Do I have a license plate hanging off me somewhere I don't know about?"

"Let's be real. People who live in Dallas do not hang out on the grassy knoll with their dog when it's ninety plus unless they've moderately lost it. See what I'm saying?"

There was some sense to what she said. "My brother and I . . ." Ian pointed toward the Book Depository, "We're from Seattle, by way of New Mexico, Arizona, Las Vegas, Bakersfield, Silverlake, etc., etc., etc., etc. FYI . . . we're musicians. We're crashing with a guy who's gonna take us to this area on Commerce where they have all the clubs."

"Deep Elum."

"There you go."

Giv was sitting in the girl's lap, getting the total treatment, the head rubs, the back scratching. "I work and live up there," she said to Ian by way of talking to Giv. "I'm an artist, at least I'm trying to be . . . cartoons, animation, graphic novels. But I do body art at a place off Commerce. It's called 'The Body Politique.' See, I learned young, that eating and indoor plumbing were absolute necessities that had to be worked for. By the way," she said to Giv, "what's your name?"

"His name is Giv. G-I-V."

"I like that." Then she angled her head toward Giv, and while he licked her ear, she acted as if she were talking to him. "My name? My name is Ruthie . . . Ruthie Ruth. I know, I know." She had an arm draped around Giv's back while she went on, "I liked Ruthie . . . and I liked Ruth. I couldn't decide between the two, so, I named myself both. How did I get to do that? Easy . . . I ran away from home when I was thirteen and took up a new name. Oh . . . I'll tell you about that another time. By the way . . . Your friend over there. Does he have a name?"

"My younger brother's name is Ian," said Jem.

Ruthie looked up. Jem approached with the sun over his shoulder so she had to squint.

"I'm Jem," he said.

"I'm only a year younger," said Ian.

"But it's a crucial year," added Jem.

Wherever the conversation might have gone, it wasn't now. Ruthie stood. "I love a good catfight but . . . I gotta get to work."

Ian told his brother, "She works up on Commerce, where the clubs are and all those hipster shops."

"Deep Elum?"

"That's it." Ruthie pointed to the Book Depository. "How was the sixth floor?"

Jem looked her over curiously.

"I told her," said Ian.

"Okay . . . I see. There's a vibe up there," he said, "very . . ."

He looked back at the building, and the corner window where history had taken that shadowy turn. He moved his hands in a push-and-pull fashion. "It had me thinking . . . very intense thinking."

"Hopefully just thinking, and not plotting," said Ian.

"A dagger to my heart, brother. A dagger to my heart."

"I got to go," said Ruthie. She gave the dog one last good rub of affection, "I hope to see you again," she told Giv.

She started away. Jem called out, "You want a ride?"

She didn't look back. "Right now . . . I feel like walking."

The brothers watched her saunter down the grassy knoll and swing the canvas satchel over a shoulder. Talk about channeling the imagination.

Ian shouted after her, "The Body Politique, right?"

Without looking, she raised a hand and gave him the thumbs-up sign.

7

BE THE MIRACLE

S EE THE DOG. *He is lying on the studio floor while the brothers prep for the auditions Stoner has set up with the people in the club world. They put in eighteen-hour days, no sweat. The urge to cruise Deep Elum and try to hook up with Ruthie occupies an awful lot of Ian's mind time, but he knows Jem would ride him into the ground for trying to cut loose.*

At their first audition the brothers' music didn't click with the club manager. At the second they were really on but the owner was iffy. At the third they were even better, and as a matter of fact, the owner thought the brothers had something. Unfortunately, he said they were a nine and a half, and he was hunting for a pure ten. Whatever that meant.

Jem took all forms of rejection as a personal affront. He handled these turndowns even worse, and what the freak had written in her diary was still punishing his ego. It was Jem who finally decided to cut loose for a night and hit the streets on his own. Before Jem left, Ian made it clear—no night prowls. Jem cupped an ear as if he were stone-cold deaf.

Once Jem had done his disappearing act, Ian took Giv and trekked out on foot for Deep Elum. The Body Politique was a good-sized storefront with an upstairs, on a block of two-story brick buildings that had been sand-blasted back into style. It was a weekend night and there were plenty of comings and goings, so he just slipped in with Giv to look for Ruthie.

The walls of the shop were a tour of inkwork styles. You want flash, you could go flash. You want *Kill Bill* or *Crumb*, the graphic novel approach, stars and stripes, total rebellion, politics, social commentary? It was freedom of the flesh here.

No sooner was he in the shop than Giv started pulling toward a beaded doorway marked *Private*. An employee over at the mag rack approached to tell him, "You got to take the dog out," just as Ian asked for Ruthie. The fella said she was working and repeated, "You have to take the dog out."

Ian said, "Sure," but as the employee turned, he let loose of Giv's leash and the dog was off, and those beaded strands were clacking like a rack of pool balls on the break.

The employee was none too happy and voiced it, and a moment later there's a female shrieking, "Ahhhhh," then "Giv." Next thing a hoisted Giv in Ruthie's arms was coming through the beads.

She spotted Ian, "Hey, listen," she said, "I have this one inking to finish, then I'm thinking, Giv and I might go out. You want to join us?"

⁓

THEY SWUNG INTO Elum. It was a weekend night and the sidewalks glowed like a fairground with light from the store-front windows. There was music drifting from the bars as doors swung open and the wind carried with it hints of per-fume and musk and food being grilled in sidewalk cafes. The dry Texas night air made the body electric to the touch and every detail of the world seemed to be drawn more sharply.

Elum was overrun with youth, and they had to maneu-ver all that street traffic by walking close. Their bodies sidled into each other in that clumsy but enticing way, and there was Giv a little out front juking through a world of streaming cutoffs and high heels and faded jeans as only the dog can.

Ruthie pointed out Casa Loco, where she bought a Ricki Lee Jones beret and Forbidden Video—'cause she'd done some outrageous body art on one of the managers—and Sol's Taco Lounge where she'd gotten another girl who was a runaway a job bussing tables.

Ian would take Ruthie by the hand one moment to get through the havoc, and she would take his arm the next. They would steal looks at each other then steal their looks away, uneasy because neither was sure yet that they wanted the other to know something had stirred.

This is the beginning before the beginning, when the first touch of bliss strikes and you sense that the intimate designs of the universe might well be in play. Uncertain beings slowly empty their hearts, but it just as easily happens unannounced.

Ian asked if it was true that Ruthie had run away.

She confessed, "Twice, actually." The first time was right after her birthday in May when she was thirteen. She went AWOL for six months, but her parents' pleadings caused her to come home. This turned out to be just bogus weeping to save their putrid public souls, so Ruthie left again a few weeks later. That was five years and how many lives ago.

Ruthie took them to an outdoor joint where Giv would be allowed and they feasted on spicy chicken wings, chili burgers and beer. Ruthie, it turned out, was from Orlando. Her folks were closet junkies who worked at Disney World. Daddy was an artist, which is probably where she picked up the vibe. Mom was business, business, business. The world saw them as politically correct, family-values, go-to-church Americans. The short form—Disney by day, disasters after dark.

While Ruthie talked, Giv remained at her side and little could be done to distract him. She was the center of his attention, the place his eyes focused.

There was something manifest and elemental in what Ian was watching. Giv had never been like that with him. In fact, the only time he had seen Giv that way was with the woman at St. Peter's. Ian came to realize he and the dog were a polite formality—friendly, yes, but still a formality. And Ian would never have the kind of bond with Giv that he was witnessing at that moment.

It was quite a life lesson the dog was teaching him through that simple act of affection. Giv had not been taken by the brothers through love, but through self-interest, and there is an intuitive difference that the dog understands. And sitting there, so did Ian. What the dog wanted, was exactly what Ian wanted.

"You've been on your own since you were thirteen. How did you keep it together so good?"

She reached up and started to slip her shirt top off her left shoulder. "I had my bottoms. The usual suspects. But I was taught something that clicked."

She got the shirt low enough to show him artwork she had created just above her breast. Ruthie had inked it herself with the aid of a mirror. It was the melding of two images. A church seemed to be transforming itself into a human face, or was a human face turning into the architecture of a church? Beneath it were the words:

BE THE MIRACLE

After running away the second time, Ruthie tripped to New Orleans with nothing more than a leather satchel. In it was a sparse wardrobe and all her drawings. One night on the downs, she came upon a clapboard place of worship by the levee. From the side of the church, lights were strung out into the empty lot beside it. There were people milling about tables. It was a night of service with food for the poor and homeless, which she'd cruised into.

Ruthie ate with the needy. A woman spoke that night, a kindergarten teacher and social worker. Her name was Ellie but throughout the parish she was known as Mz. El. She had been written about in the *Picayune Newspaper* for helping those in need.

Mz. El had come from Jamaica as a girl. "With only the clothes on my back and the soul in my body," she'd say. "Clothes come and go," she said, "but the soul . . ."

Mz. El was nearing seventy that night and spoke to each table with the enthusiasm of a teenager. "We, as people, pray for miracles, beg for miracles, plead for miracles to better our lives, to change our lives, to affect our lives, to assuage our suffering, yet . . . would life not be best served if we became the miracle."

"She became like my grandmother," said Ruthie. "She got me a job. She had a little attic room I lived in."

"Why'd you come here?"

"I met some artists in New Orleans. One came here to work for a little company that does graphic novels. I tried to get in with them, but it didn't happen. I've been seriously thinking about going back to New Orleans."

Giv was now standing on his hind legs licking the side of Ruthie's face. "You're just too much," she said talking to the dog. She asked Ian, "Where'd you get this character?"

"He likes you a lot better than he likes me."

"That's not so."

"Yes."

"Well . . . I *am* likeable!"

Logic would suggest Ian lie about where he got the dog. Or just blow the question off completely. But he felt compelled to be honest with Ruthie even if it left him vulnerable.

"My brother stole him," said Ian.

Ruthie wasn't sure if she should be shocked or if Ian was joking and her expression said exactly that.

Ian repeated, "My brother stole him."

"From where?"

"From a woman at some motel."

She looked down at Giv. He'd sunk his head into her lap and just let it lie there. "A thing like that could break someone's heart."

"I know."

"It would mine."

Ian was completely deflated. "Mine, too."

"If your brother stole him, why didn't you give him back?"

"My brother did something that made it impossible."

"Like?"

Ian slumped down into his seat. "He robbed the woman."

Ian wanted out of there and right now. No, it was way beyond that. At the very least, he wanted to be atomized instantly.

"You see how he is with you and how he is with me. And I know why. It's because Giv knows what was done to him. That he got ripped off. And he's still cool. He still puts out the affection. He's solid, in his heart. It's like he forgave me. Then I see how he is with you, and I know why that is too. It's because of where you come from as a person. It just pours right out of your skin and you wear it. The difference is you're the right kind of love, and I'm the almost-right kind of love and the difference . . . the difference." He leaned forward and puts his hands out wide, thinking . . . "The difference between the right kind of love, and the almost-right kind is . . . well . . . the difference between a perfect chord and . . . a bum note."

[8]

Rebellion

S EE THE DOG *and the girl in silhouette. They are a perfect unity of shades just beyond the border of the restaurant lights. Ian takes a moment and just watches before he goes to join them. In that mysterious place within, he finds himself making wishes.*

They walk together in silence, and she guides them over to Commerce. He doesn't understand what, if anything, the silence means. Has he ultimately lost her with the truth?

Then, as if almost in response to his thought, she took her loose hand and slid it into the back of his belt and just held it as they walked. The street grew quieter, the pole lamps guided them with pools of light.

"I knew this would happen," she said.

"What?"

"You and me. The three of us. I imagined it when I first saw you in Dealey."

"Yeah?"

"Absolute. I'd ask you if you imagined us, but I don't want to know. Just in case you didn't. But . . . you showed. So I guess you did."

"I'm here."

"Don't tell me anymore."

"All right."

He put his arm around her.

"Finally," she whispered.

He smiled.

"Of course," she said, "I saw Giv first."

Hearing his name Giv's head arced around.

"Yeah. I'm talking about you. As a matter of fact," she told Ian, "if it hadn't been for him, I might never have noticed you."

⁓

RUTHIE HAD A CELL of a room on the second floor of the Body Politique. Two other employees lived up there in similar rooms, and they all shared a common bath. At the end of the hall was a stairwell to the roof. The roof was flat and tarred and quiet. Ian and Ruthie sat on the roof ledge and drank beer, while Giv cruised the air vents, sniffing out worlds that drifted up through the murky piping.

The night was cloudless and strewn with stars. You could look out over Deep Elum, lit for blocks, and beyond it the glass-and-steel Dallas skyline. There was a kind of majesty to it all of a sudden. A world there and poised just for you.

"What's that song?" asked Ruthie. "When I get . . .

something, something, something, something, something
. . . up on the roof."

Ian leaned back and grinned. A singer she was not. "I
don't think the song has quite that many 'somethings.'"

She gave him a slap. "You know what I'm talking about,
right?"

"I know the song." He actually could riff the first few
lines. "My mother," he said, "did that song in her lounge
act. She ran away from home to be a singer on those cruise
ships. You know, music to enjoy a coma by."

Ruthie threw her head back and laughed out loud, and
just like that Giv was over there and it was the three of
them now. Ian noticed Ruthie grew more thoughtful,
then serious. She was stroking Giv's head when she asked,
"Why did your brother steal Giv? He's not into dogs. I
picked that up in Dealey. He is nowhere."

Ian put his beer down and just sat there. "He had his
reasons."

"You don't want to tell me."

"I wanted Giv and asked the lady who had him to sell
him. She was cool. She did not *sell* dogs. Giv was named
after his father, who died. They were tight. I told Jem."
That was the simple answer, but it was not the soul at the
center of the truth. To go there, you had to go back to
Morrison.

"My father," Ian began, "among his many talents," and
Ian stroked the word "talent" with bitterness, "trained
guard dogs."

Ian detailed his father's sinister side of using "his boys" as attack dummies, and how the old man named each dog for a sixties rock star. Morrison for Jim Morrison of "The Doors."

"This is the end, my only friend, the end," he added.

Ruthie asked, "What are you saying?"

Everything had disappeared for Ian. The Dallas skyline, Deep Elum, the rooftop, Ruthie. He was staring at Giv, but he was not seeing him. He was seeing into him as if Giv were this corridor of time that took him back to the black substance of his life, when it was drawn and quartered.

Ian had never told the story. Not to a relative, not to a buddy, nor a girlfriend. Morrison had been a German shepherd. Ultimately cool. You told him a thing once and his brain was like a PC. He had it down. He loved to hang with "the boys." His thing was bandanas and handkerchiefs. You left one of those around, you didn't close a bureau drawer, Morrison was in the backyard at full tilt boogie with it streaming out of his mouth. The chase flag, baby. Catch me if you can.

Morrison was never to be sold. He was the old man's promo reel, his sales pitch, calling card, and the Oscar goes to . . . He was the extension of their father's dashed impulses and controlled fury. Or as their old man described him—he's my law and order.

Now Jem and the old man had lived in what you would at best call a standoff. Their confrontations went to extremes as a matter of course. The old man was strict precision and didn't waste a drop of sympathy, so when Jem was given an order and threw the old man that magazine-cover-mugshot stare meant to set him off, you could expect violence. This particular fight had taken place in the living room with Ian clinging to the background and crying as he watched his brother get all blooded up. At one point the father looked away and at Ian and yelled, "You're f——n' wallpaper, you know that. Wimp—wallpaper."

Because of those few seconds when the old man had looked away from Jem, all their lives would be changed forever. Jem had grabbed a mug off the coffee table and flung it. It was the first time he had answered violence with violence. There was a hard thud where it scored cheekbone. Their father stood there stunned. What had begun as a teardrop of blood soon became a long thin stream of it down his unshaven face. He neither did anything, nor said anything. He just walked to the kitchen then out of the house.

Ian then went over to Jem and used his shirtsleeve to wipe the blood from around his brother's nose.

"Don't cry," said Jem. "Don't give him the satisfaction."

The kitchen door had opened and slammed shut. Their father was coming back. Only this time he had Morrison. He not only had the dog, he had a gun wedged down in his belt.

"Tough kid, huh."

"Don't say anything, Jem."

The father meant to bait the boy out. The boy meant to outman the man, and the man would use whatever means to see the boy undone. It is the way a perpetual hell is created.

The father came around the couch with Morrison at his side. And like nothing, like absolutely nothing, the father ordered Morrison to attack, and take Jem down.

Ruthie could not absorb what she was hearing. And Ian was trembling as he went on, his hands visibly shaking as he relived it for her.

"Morrison loved Jem," said Ian, "and he didn't understand. He looked at my father and he looked at Jem and his ears were back and he was ordered again but he wouldn't do it."

Ian began to cry. "No matter how my old man railed Morrison would not obey *that* command and so my father, man, oh man, my father, he went after Jem himself. He was beating my brother and I was crying like I am now only worse." And as soon as Ian said that, he began to unravel and his crying came up in choky bursts.

Giv knew something was wrong. Since Ian had slid from the ledge and was sitting on the tar roof, Giv cradled up into him and started licking Ian's face, at the tears, and he even started to make sounds, to talk, as if the wounds inside one were inside the other.

Ian looked up tear-faced. "Morrison knew something was wrong. That what was happening was wrong, bad wrong, and he went after my father. Oh, yeah. He got hold of my father's arm, and he was trying to pull my old man off Jem. He was—"

Ian pounded a fist into his opened hand. "Morrison wasn't trying to hurt him. Only stop him."

Ian's jaw muscles were starting to convulse, and he had to clamp his lower lip with his teeth as if the ship of state that was his whole being would come entirely apart if he did not. He was incapable of speaking, so he made his hand into a gun shape and fired.

"Your father shot Morrison? He shot his own dog?"

Ian took hold of Giv and buried his head in the dog's neck and chest. "I'm sorry for what's been done to you. Please. I'm sorry."

WITH ONE CANDLE, Ruthie's room was shadows and swimmy shapes along the ceiling. There was a mattress on a box spring on the floor, and that is where Ian lay. His emotions had subsided. Ruthie sat on the mattress with her back against the wall. Giv lay close beside Ian, so close in fact his head rested on Ian's stomach. It was the first time since he'd had Giv that Giv had shown him that much affection.

"We're gonna hook up, aren't we?"

"I hope," said Ian.

She liked his intonation.

"I drink beer some," she said. "With pizza it's a must. I do shooters from time to time. I don't do drugs of any kind anymore, and I won't be around them. That's a no. And sex? Remember what you told me about Giv. The right kind of love and the almost-right kind . . ."

"The perfect chord or the bum note."

"I've done the bum note. I want a permanent union, not a maybe thing, a could be thing. Let's see how it fits or feels or . . . what the hey. I was shown—be the miracle—is not a slogan. It's a way of life."

"I get what you're saying."

"And it's all right."

She paused and waited.

Ian sat up slightly. "I'm totally with you."

He put a hand out and she reached for it. He pulled her toward him and she leaned down and they kissed. He ran a hand back through her hair; she responded with fingers along his boyish stubble.

Everyone who was ever young knows that first kiss, the one with someone you sense your life history and heart will be overwhelmingly tied to. It is one of the cherished possessions of youth, that steals every part of your body with the force of gravity, leaving all substance outside of you to disappear.

⌐

THEY WERE THERE with music drifting in from some room down the hall; the candlelight's magic across their faces; moonlight framed by the window; and that perfect, quiet breeze.

There is only this tiny island with the warmth of their skin and the wonders of passion. There, all wounds fall away. There, doubts are conquered, as are fears and feelings of exile. There, loneliness is just a word. There, the smallest moments turned into dreams, living and breathing and stretching far out into tomorrows. And you are suddenly, completely connected to the universe, because you are no longer you, you are another you, one who has become part of a "we," that exists through and because of the other.

⁓

THE CANDLE WAS guttering out, the last of its magic trailing across the ceiling, until Ruthie lit another. She was sitting on the bed doing a sketch. She wouldn't let Ian see. Giv was asleep on her lap. Ian sat on the open windowsill with his legs up and looking out into the Dallas night.

He and Jem would not be long for this place, then what? And if Ruthie headed back to New Orleans, what then? Her traveling with them would be out of the question. Become the miracle—was not Jem's kind of motto.

Gradually Ian began to question what would be the form of his destiny, circumstance or choice. He felt a crossroads coming, and he knew in any confrontation with his brother, there would be no place for an imposter. His brother had always been the stronger, tougher anyway, and Ian, he felt he was, as his father would say, "wallpaper."

Ruthie stopped drawing momentarily, and from what seemed out of nowhere she said, "What was Jim Morrison famous for?"

"Jim Morrison?"

"Yes."

"He was lead singer for 'The Doors.' 'This is the end friend, my only friend . . .'"

"No. What I'm asking is, like so many of those sixties rockers, what was he famous for?"

"Being brilliant, outrageous, a druggie."

"Rebellious," she said. "He was famous for being rebellious. You see where I'm going?"

"No."

"Your father named Morrison right, but he didn't get it. Your father probably thought he could train Morrison to be the mindless and obedient robot. Do exactly as told, no thinking. He probably thought Morrison couldn't think, he was just a dog. And your father was all-powerful, and the all-powerful would be obeyed. But . . .

"Morrison fooled him. He exercised free will and chose what was right. He rebelled." Ruthie looked down at Giv. "Where'd your gang get that free will? Did God put it there?"

9

BROTHER AGAINST BROTHER

SEE THE DOG *in the drawing. He is a hipster version of Giv wearing shades and sitting in a director's chair, human style, with legs outstretched and getting inked by a feral Ruthie. In the drawing, she has shaved out a heart shape of hair on Giv's shoulder and that is where she is creating. Now, that in itself is a part of a larger drawing. It is a heart-shaped tattoo being inked on Ian's shoulder by Ruthie as he sits in a director's chair, with legs outstretched and wearing the same shades as Giv. And Giv, he is sitting in the background reading a book. The title: "Morrison—The Rebel."*

In the morning Ruthie drove "the boys" home. She had an old VW bug with a crank sunroof and an engine that sounded like a lawnmower.

Jem was in the studio but could see the drop off through the screen door—Ian leaning down into the open sunroof and kissing Ruthie goodbye. There was nothing vague about all that body language.

Ian was tacking the sketch up to the bulletin board in the guesthouse when Jem closed in. He got a pretty good look at it over Ian's shoulder, and he didn't like what he saw. It had that "I'm so into us" vibe.

"Won the lottery, huh?"

"She tells me if it wasn't for Giv she might never even have noticed me up in Dealey. I love you, Giv."

"Well, see what a good thing I did ripping that dog off."

Ian dropped down on the couch beside Giv who'd already taken up his usual spot. Jem wasn't getting an answer from his brother, not any answer. Ian just sat there putting all his attention into Giv as if he hadn't even heard Jem.

"Do not blow me off, you hear!"

"It still doesn't sit well with me, all right."

"Then give that thing back."

"He is not a thing."

"I'm serious, when we get out of here, which will be soon, we can cruise on over to Cemeteryville and dump him."

Ian had taken off a boot and he dropped it down. "I'm gonna grab a shower, because in the shower . . ." his voice rose and rose . . . "I won't be able to hear you."

He stood and started toward the bathroom.

"I didn't steal from the woman."

Ian stopped and turned. His brother had a trigger-finger smirk. "You just have to play games, don't you, Jem?"

"I-did-not-steal-from-that-freak."

Ian took his shirt off. "Where you going with this?"

"I knew you wanted the dog, so I made it easy for you to keep him. Now, I'm making it easy for you to give him back. 'Cause that's the way you like it, when decisions are easy. Easy, meaning someone makes them for you."

Ian flung the shirt at his brother's feet.

"Is that your version of a confrontation . . . baby brother?"

"Maybe it's my way of avoiding one."

"Ahhhh. . . . The wallpaper talks."

"Jem! You lied to me 'cause you wanted to hurt that woman, right? Now you're telling me the truth, if it is the truth. Why? Because you want to hurt someone. Who is the someone this time, Jem? Me?"

"What's with that drawing . . . 'Morrison—The Rebel.'"

"I told Ruthie about Morrison 'cause it is a heavy piece of who we are. And who we aren't."

~

THE SHOWER WENT ON, the sound so loud through the paper-thin walls Jem was reminded how much his life was not his own. He stood staring at Giv lying there on the couch, his head listing upon the armrest. The dog paid Jem no mind.

He glanced at Ruthie's drawing. Ian's words were like

poison—*she told me, if it wasn't for Giv she might not even have noticed me up in Dealey.*

That dog was the seed of a disaster. Yeah. Jem tried to dismiss the idea but there was a certain inevitability to it that had him by the underpinnings. Even that drawing belied the obvious. Jem was living out a precarious stability, and he knew it.

The chickie voodoo, with all its visual suggestion. High school hypnosis posing as true love. With a dog, no less, as the all-American centerpiece. His brother, the babe, and a dog.

Jem, man. Don't you see it coming? Let's take a ride around the American psyche and come up with some sort of profound commercial that clearly speaks of deep interpretation. There's a lawn and picket fence in every heart, just don't forget the older brother, with the rifle in an open window.

Jem walked up to Giv and cracked him right across the head. He hit him so hard Giv could hardly keep from going over the edge of the couch. For Jem, it was a moment of terrible joy to see the muscles up through the dog's legs and shoulders shivering with fear. He felt ashamed again for hurting the dog, but there was also an exhilaration at having such an effect on something smaller and weaker.

In those few seconds one gets to be what one is not, and at the same time, one gets to be exactly what one is. In both cases, the person is a distinct coward in disguise.

Jem knew it about himself and it disgusted him, which

made him angrier and more ashamed. And that anger and shame demanded he act. You get to be your father, child. Repeat the misery of your life long enough, and maybe it will go away. These are the kinds of thoughts that failures are made from.

He went to backhand Giv, but he hesitated for just long enough to really anchor for full impact, and those few seconds would change all their lives forever. Giv saw and understood. Be it violence or rage. The dark side of the human bloodline. Dogs have known those scents since the beginning of time. They were there when the first blood was shed, and they will be there when the last is shed.

Before the hand could register, Giv struck. You could hear the growl coming up the throat and through a flash of teeth. Jem cursed out and backpedaled, and Giv was up now and he leaned out from the couch snarling.

Jem tried to shake off the pain, and he had every intention of turning some ultimate wrath upon that dog, when the bathroom door jerked open and there was Ian soaking wet and naked. "What the hell is—"

Jem held out a bloody hand and forearm.

Ian yelled for Giv to quiet, but the dog was tautly focused on Jem and would not quiet. Brother asked brother, "What did you do?"

"What did I do?"

Ian shouted, "You!"

"I was going to reach for—"

Ian swatted away his brother's hand, "Bulls—t."

⸺

AT THE TIME, "Trees" was a nightclub in the 2700 block
of Elm. Their band auditions were open to the public.
Stoner had arranged one. There was also a club owner
from Memphis that Stoner had quietly called.

The brothers did their best to keep tension in check
while they rehearsed. Impassioned antagonists was how
Stoner would describe them. Each day he hoped to see a
change, but it was becoming a permanent state.

You might have thought their music would suffer. On
the contrary, their personal drama seemed to intensify
the songs, and bring out new depths in the lyrics. After
each work session, Ian would split for Deep Elum. Since
that morning in the shower he also made sure Giv was
never alone with Jem. As a matter of fact, as the audition approached and work hours grew longer, Giv stayed
exclusively with Ruthie.

Ian and Ruthie had just gotten takeout from a joint
named, of all things, "The Angry Dog," when Ian asked
her what New Orleans was like.

She queried, "To visit?"

"To live."

"You and your brother?"

"No."

As soon as they actually started to delve into the possibility of going there together and cranking up a life, Ian
had not only a deep sense of relief, but of actual liberation.

He would no longer have to exist with limited emotional expectations.

The hard part, and this Ruthie understood instinctively, would be Ian actually splitting from Jem. It is one thing to define your intentions and quite another to deliver on them. But of course, sometimes youth's most valuable ally is youth itself. The divinity of pure energy goes a long way toward accomplishing purpose.

For the audition, Ruthie put out word so there'd be a favorable audience. She bribed an assistant manager so she and Giv could be backstage by the alley door during the audition.

The brothers demonstrated their talent. Execution and passion, plus originality. But that was not enough. Sometimes chance sadly overshadows talent.

After the audition, Stoner asked Ian if he could talk with him privately. Ian found himself on the roof patio of the Green Tea Room with the owner of that club in Memphis. Stoner saw the brothers were having troubles and decided if they were doing a Lennon-and-McCartney, he would try and hook up with the more talented one. So, he clandestinely sent out Ian's solo tapes about a week before the audition.

The club owner had a studio in Memphis and was looking for an inspired guitarist to help a Christian band get their first CD together. The band was a well-reviewed comer and who knows where the gig could take Ian?

The excitement Ian felt at the possible life unfolding

before him was measured against the prevailing one unraveling behind him. Jem had no idea of Ian's plan the day after the audition when Ian was packing Ruthie's sparse belongings into her VW bug.

The plan was simple. She would take Giv and drive to Mz. El's house in St. Bernard's Parish. Ian would confront Jem, explain how he was breaking with him, weather whatever storm came out of it, rent a van, load up his equipment and head to Memphis for the recording session. Then it would be a straight run down 55 to New Orleans to hook up with Ruthie.

Ian knew how short-tempered and vindictive Jem could be, so when he had the studio to himself he collected up copies of all the tapes the brothers had worked on together, plus his solo tapes. What Ian did not realize was that he had taken some of Jem's solo sessions that had been mislabeled. He gave all these to Ruthie, as protection, for her to take in the VW.

There came that moment when the Volks was loaded and Giv was hunkered down in the shotgun seat and panting lightly and it was time. The world was out there waiting, children, in all its imperfect beauty, to embrace you.

They kissed and held each other and kissed again and Ian whispered, "Two wings of time are neatly tied."

Ruthie suddenly did not want to let him go. Even a temporary farewell can feel like the wind whirling in a courtyard.

The world went on as usual in broad daylight as Ian

watched Ruthie drive off. He waved and her arm came up through the open sunroof to wave back.

Make me see and feel and remember this day always, he thought. He kept watching as best he could as the Volks slipped into traffic with its engine stressing through each shift, and there was Giv, head projecting out of the shotgun window.

Ruthie held on to him through the rearview mirror. *Dear Ian, my portrait of tenderness.* Love is beyond mystery or truth; it is the full possession of one's self that even the contact of bodies cannot fully encompass. Love overwhelms thirst, it determines all.

And just like that, she turned off Commerce and was gone and Ian was alone on the sun hot, Dallas sidewalk. He felt such an emptiness. *I am a shadow without a name.*

⁓

JEM RETURNED TO Stoner's house to find Ian sitting on the couch in Giv's old spot, and near the door a couple of packed suitcases.

"Should I gather Dallas is done for us?"

"Not for us, Jem. Me."

As Jem moved through the room, there was a stony indifference that Ian did not quite expect.

"So, I don't even get the standard 'I've been thinking about it.' You just hammer me with this," pointing to the suitcases, "visual touch."

"I didn't know any other way. See, Jem, I'm not emotionally equipped to handle you."

"All the work, all the years, all the effort. All the . . . dot, dot, dot . . . is bound for Dumpster city."

"I need a new direction."

"You need something, all right."

Jem started to thoughtfully pace. "Where you heading from here?"

"New Orleans."

"Isn't that where . . . ?" he jerked his hand toward Ruthie's sketch.

"Yes."

"What about—"

"Giv is with her now."

"Doin' the nest thing, huh. You know, if you don't be careful, you're gonna grow up to be an AT&T commercial. How you gonna get there?"

"Where?"

"New Orleans."

"I was gonna rent a van. Bring my guitars, whatever equipment you thought okay. I'd give you first choice on synthesizers, computers, speakers . . ."

"What about money?"

"I got a few miles left on a Visa. And Ruthie will lend me some."

"Save the money. I'll take you to New Orleans."

Ian did not know quite how to deal with this. His brother was gravestone matter-of-fact.

"You thought I was gonna go bad-assed on you. Right . . . ? Wrong, brother."

Jem could express more with a look than all the words Ian knew put together. He started playing an illusory guitar, head down, back bowed, as if his whole body was bent under some pallid weight. He riffed a little Concrete Blonde: "It is complete now, two wings of time are neatly tied."

Then, Jem said, "I'll take you to where you need to go. New Orleans, right. I'll show you what a real brother is made of."

10

FUN, FUN, FUN

"MIRA PERRO," shouted the boy. "Mira perro." There were a couple of kids in a rattly pickup, and one was pointing at a Volks that was hauling past.

Riding shotgun and getting a head full of wind was Giv. He caught sight of the kids waving and calling to him and his muzzle tipped out the window with what looked, to the kids, could only be a grin. One boy put up a power fist and yelled, "Perro," and then the Volks was history.

Ruthie was kicking it down through Angelina County on I-69. Destination—Beaumont, which is where she and Giv would cross into Louisiana. I-69 is part of the Trans-Texas Corridor and famous for having more highway signs stolen than any road in America—the reason, doubtless needs little explanation.

The girl's whole being literally hummed. And if you asked Ruthie how she felt, she would have told you her heart just bouqueted with happiness, with this unbreakable thread of unspoiled emotion. She couldn't kiss Giv enough, or talk out her dreams for all of them enough. He put a paw on her shoulder as she went on as if in total concert, reminding her the wounded terrain of our past determines nothing.

They had just crossed the Neches River when through the rearview, Ruthie saw waves of chrome trembling in the heat that had begun to rise up out of the asphalt and coalesce into a shimmering armada of decked-out choppers, followed by a pickup on oversized wheels. You could hear the sound of their engines coming on fast, and Giv stood now with his front paws on the back of the seat and his head up through the open sunroof, body stretched all it could from withers to croup. A living periscope focused on these mounted riders coming out of a sea of Texas heat.

And above the growl of the choppers now was music. Strapped down in the bed of that pickup was a huge boombox, and as the riders flared around the Volks, Ruthie could see they were all girls, girls not much older than herself, and they had this hiply fugitive look that said they could be packing pistols as easily as perfume.

Now, Giv had hauled himself up as high as possible and he was a barking machine as the riders swept past. One of the girls on the back of a Harley pointed at Giv and said something to the driver, and Ruthie saw that bike flank another and the girl was pointing back at the Volks and pretty soon that girl waved for Ruthie to "come on."

Ruthie had no idea what the girls had in mind, but she gunned that engine till it was going all out and the riders let her catch up and the truck slipped across lanes and was right behind them.

Suddenly there was a blast of music out of that boombox and you could almost feel the asphalt lift. It was pure guitar rock-and-roll with some hip, chickie band doing their version of an old Beach Boys classic, "Fun, Fun, Fun."

They'd done the classic, alright, but they'd gone the Beach Boys one better. The harmonies were hotter, the voices brassier, and the lyrics, well . . . It wasn't their daddy's station wagon they'd copped for a run to the malt shop. It was a chrome monster the girls were riding, and the pink slips were theirs, and they were hot on the trail of some reckless abandon. It was this generation's fun, fun, fun, with a chick-lit flavor.

The chopper with the girl on the back slowed a bit more, so it was now just on the Volks' shotgun flank, and the girl pulled this wild blue bandana from her jean pocket and held it out so the wind raggedly snapped it. She was leaning into the Volks and teasing Giv with it, and there he was trying to leap just enough, just that little bit enough, to get a mouthful of cloth.

The chopper edged in closer yet, so close, in fact, the inside of the Volks was filling with the heat from its engine. The girl leaned all the way out so she was practically touching the windshield, and that bandana was going like the electrocuted tail of a snake, bare inches, maybe not even inches, from Giv's snapping teeth.

The girl leaned a little more yet and Giv stretched what was left of his body to stretch and he could feel the tip of that bandana insulting his nose. The girl leaned farther yet and was so far out from the side of that chopper, Ruthie could see the smallest details on the rings the girl was wearing.

And that little bit was enough. Giv made one nose-lunge and got it. But the girl did not let go. No way. And there they all were—this caravan of chrome beauties and a monster mash truck and a Volks with no hubs and a paint job that predated the Mayflower doing a bad ninety through the barren heat, while Giv and the girl were having this tug-of-war.

Just like that the girl let go and the loose end of the bandana lashed up around Giv's head, and poking up out of the sunroof, he looked like a pirate wearing a wild-blue, cloth eyepatch.

The pitch of creativity was happening in Ruthie, though she did not know it—she wouldn't for a few hours yet, anyway. It was part of the same volcanic energy that had birthed Marlon Brando, the biker, in *The Wild One,* who when asked in a California town, "What are you rebelling against?" answered, "What have you got?" It had birthed James Dean and a game of chicken on the Pacific bluffs in *Rebel Without a Cause.* It spawned *The Grapes of Wrath* and

Dean Moriarity in *On The Road* and Jack Nicholson on the back of a chopper wearing a football helmet while the Byrds sang, "The river, it flows to the sea, and wherever that river goes, that's where I want to be."

It gave us *The Call of the Wild* and *Sullivan's Travels* and *Travels With Charley* and *The Electric Kool Aid Acid Test* and *Vanishing Point* and *Route 66* and Bob Dylan singing, "Where you want this killing done? God said out on Highway 61." There's Johnny Appleseed and Ishmael, though his road was the sea, and *The Leatherstocking Tales* and *It Happened One Night* and *Superman* and *The Incredible Journey* and John Wayne in *The Searchers* promising he would find his kidnapped niece "just as sure as the turning of the earth," and Robert Frost's "The Road Less Traveled."

MZ. EL LIVED just south of Fleur de Lis Park in the same house where she had raised four boys and cared for her ailing husband until he died. One son was now a teacher in Detroit; another ran a daycare center in Miami; the third was a policeman who lived at the end of the very same block. The fourth—he had died in Vietnam at the age of nineteen. He was Mz. El's unfinished life, and in large measure, why she had such an affinity for young people, lost or in need. Mz. El would often say, "Sometimes just a crevice of light is all that's necessary for the promise to shine through."

Ruthie had been e-mailing Mz. El all along about Ian and Giv and their litany of hopes, and now when Ruthie called to say she was about an hour out of New Orleans, the old woman found herself sitting on the front porch in the evening light like an expectant grandmother.

When headlights swept into the driveway and a horn honked Mz. El made a deep and grateful sigh.

One can tell how happy someone is by the light that emanated from the earthly wrapping around their soul, and Mz. El had never seen Ruthie so filled with happiness. She skipped right up the porch steps and the two hugged and damn if the old woman didn't cry a bit.

Then Mz. El got a good look at Giv, whom she already knew from a mountain of e-mails. Mz. El gave that dog's flank such a hearty thumping his head jostled and she treated him to a biscuit she had bought especially for his arrival, but Giv caught sight of something staring at him from inside the screen door that grabbed his attention a lot more.

It turned out Mz. El had taken in a neighbor's cat while they were on vacation. The cat was named Bullet, and Mz. El said the name was appropriate as the cat had a take-no-prisoners nasty streak, and it was going to be something to see how Bullet would share the space with Giv.

It took all of one minute to find out, 'cause as soon as the screen door was opened and Giv started approaching Bullet with a kind of laissez-faire curiosity, the cat's back arched up and he took one good swipe at Giv's nose. The dog howled and the cat took off, as cats will, and like some acrobatic Zorro, a second later he was safely up on the breakfront.

⟜

Mz. El sat at the dining room table while Ruthie called Ian. She was looking over some sketches Ruthie had started at a truck stop on her way to New Orleans. That crew of girl bikers had given her a rush of ideas, and after splitting from them, Ruthie pulled off the road while she was still fresh with inspiration.

When Ruthie returned from the kitchen where she had made the call, Mz. El noticed her expression. Ruthie was one of those people who had cornered the market on what you feel is how you look.

"What is it?" asked Mz. El.

"I don't know. I called Ian twice today but he hasn't answered his cell. I left him two messages, but he's answered neither one."

"You did say it would be difficult with his brother."

"Ian called me around noon and said his brother had offered to drive him here. Ian hadn't told him about the job in Memphis. He didn't want to . . . upset him, or make him feel bad. So, he decided to let Jem drive him here and split for Memphis once he was gone."

Mz. El tried to be reassuring. "When you're old, the hours seem like minutes, when you're young, the minutes seem like hours. It doesn't work out great either way, does it? And by the way, it might be emotionally a lot more difficult than you even suspect for Ian to break with his brother. He may need his own emotional quiet time to get through the trip."

Mz. El now made Ruthie tell her about the drawings. She showed Mz. El what she'd caught of the girl bikers on her cell phone camera and how it had inspired her.

⁓

IAN DID NOT call Ruthie that night. Mz. El could hear Ruthie pacing in the attic overhead and leaving message after message on Ian's cell phone.

Later she came downstairs to find Ruthie on the front porch in the dark crying into Giv's shoulder. Mz. El readily saw Giv was now anchor and living ballast. God, she felt, had worked a secret miracle, for Ruthie might well need him as an anchor for runaway emotions.

By next morning it became clear something needed to be done. Mz. El asked Ruthie if she could contact the brother. At first, Ruthie believed she could not, but it turned out Jem's cell phone number was written on the CD boxes Ian had given her for safe keeping.

She called Jem and, of all things, he answered. Nervously, she asked about Ian. Jem was surprised it was her; you might say he was even disconcerted.

He told her he had dropped Ian off in Tyler, Texas. They had been at a coffee shop called the Arcadia when Ian opened up to him about the gig in Memphis. Both decided it would be best to make a complete split right there. Jem told Ruthie he last saw Ian gathering up his belongings on the sidewalk just up from the Arcadia and about a block from the bus station.

For Ruthie the inexplicable now magnified into a true state of emergency. If what Jem had said was not suspect, Ian had either blown her off or befallen some tragedy.

She looked at the box with all Ian's tapes and asked Mz. El, "Even if he decided to dump me, his dreams are there. He wouldn't just . . . leave *them*."

Mz. El took it upon herself to contact her son. Rafer came by the house about an hour later in his squad car. Rafer knew the girl well, and his mother had her detail out events. What he heard didn't feel right, though he said nothing. When he got back to the precinct house, he started making calls.

He checked the hospitals in and around Tyler to see if Ian had been admitted. When that proved a dead end, he contacted the local police and sheriff's department. That also proved a dead end, so he started the machinations of filing a missing person's report.

11

MISSING

THE SNAPSHOT OF *the boy, the girl and the dog is the only picture of Ian that Ruthie has. It was taken by a friend of hers outside the Body Politique just two days before she'd left Dallas. Rafer makes copies which he gets off to the appropriate authorities in Tyler. He tells his mother privately, "If this is some form of self-imposed disappearance, for whatever reason . . . drugs, another girl, we can assume one thing, he will show up for the job in Memphis which is just days away. If he doesn't . . ."*

Ruthie herself had brought this up. She and Mz. El were sitting at dinner, though Ruthie had hardly eaten since that first night. The old woman knew too well that there was no space so desolate as being young and in love and believing you've been cast aside. "Of course," said Ruthie, picking at her food, "It would be better that than . . ."

The goodness in Ruthie never ceased to move the old woman. Only now, Ruthie clung to it as one would a life raft. They sat on the porch together one night with Giv and drank beer, the Louisiana moon, full and luminous, across the stretch of canal just blocks away.

The old woman sat with her arm around Ruthie's shoulder and watched as she poured a glass of beer, then let Giv have a few licks of foam.

"He's always liked beer," said Ruthie. "Ian told me, he was that way with the woman Jem stole Giv from."

As much to make a point as to try to help Ruthie forget for a little while, Mz. El started in on a story about when she was young and in love for the first time.

"When I first saw him, he was in uniform. He was tall and lean and had beautiful skin. He had just finished his service, and when he came over and introduced himself I became every cliché that ever was. Unchain my heart and soul. I could feel my ankles pulsing all the way to Arabia. Now I can't even find my ankles.

"We were that instant. And did we have plans. I would teach school, and he would open a little restaurant or coffee shop and we'd have children and, well . . . he did everything he said he would, but he did it with my cousin. Ran off and married her."

"You never told me this."

"I'm telling you now. Was I broken up. 'The queen of brooding waters.' That's what my mother would call me. Well, one Saturday I was going to confession. Though I did not have much to confess, unfortunately. I was sitting in a pew waiting my turn and quietly crying into my handkerchief. Well, when it was my turn, I went into the confessional, but I was so into my own misery that I walked right in on someone giving *their* confession. Stumbled right into them in that little dark cubicle. I was so ashamed I ran out of the church and all the way home. I didn't go back to church for two weeks.

"Well, one day I was in a little coffee shop called Papa Lou's. I was in a booth alone, and suddenly this young man just sits down at my table. I look up and he's staring at me and smiling. I am still the queen of brooding waters and I say to this young man, 'What are you doing? There's tables everywhere.' And he just keeps smiling and I say, 'What are you smiling at? If you think you're gonna sit down here and . . .'

"'What's your name?' he said. 'I'm not going to give you my name,' I said. And he says, 'Well, that's the least you can do since you already heard my confession.'"

"No," said Ruthie.

"And you know who he was?"

Mz. El held up her left hand and touched the finger with the wedding band she still wore.

"No?" It made Ruthie smile. "I understand what you're saying, mama."

⟶

IAN DID NOT show in Memphis, nor was he heard from by anyone. Rafer tracked the boys' parents to notify them.

The father had an intense disinterest in his sons, but the mother flew to Tyler immediately. Jem retold his story to the police, and what he said matched the version he had given Rafer.

It was during that period of days the police validated Jem's story with a shop owner's. Her business was just up and around the corner from the Arcadia. She had seen a boy unloading suitcases from a van in front of her shop about a week earlier. Hours later, at closing time, she'd noticed the suitcases were still there on the sidewalk. She took them into her shop and called the authorities. She could not be absolutely certain, but the boy in the snapshot taken out front of the Body Politique certainly could have been the one.

Of course, Jem and Ian looked much alike and were near the same age.

The question to Jem was, "Why did you drop Ian there and not take him to the Greyhound station less than two blocks away?"

Jem's answer, "I offered, but this is what Ian wanted. Maybe he just split and said the hell with all of it."

A boy and two guitars missing. In his suitcases were nothing of value. Had he taken his guitars and gotten on a bus, or hitched a ride? Had he left it all behind for some unknown destructive reason?

There was no evidence to contradict Jem's story. The shop owner had said about the same, but when Ian's mother called Rafer to inform him of this, she confessed she did not fully believe Jem.

She also talked to Ruthie. "I saw a snapshot of you and Ian. You look like quite a lovely girl." She wanted also to say that judging from her phone conversation with Ruthie, she sensed Ian and she would have been very happy together. But, that felt of such finality, she said nothing.

⁓

RUTHIE WENT INTO a tailspin. She spent her days with Giv at the park or walking the 17th Street Canal to the shores of Lake Pontchartrain, where Giv could chase herons while she existed under the tyrannical rule of the imprisoned mind. Inside oneself is a blue land indeed, when one's dreams seem to have been destroyed.

Yes, being human can be an impossible habit to break, and as Mz. El watched her girl slip further and further into a malaise, she took all the boxes of Ruthie's drawings and put them on a charcoal grill in the backyard. When Ruthie and Giv returned from another round of diminishing solace Mz. El showed her this pyre of her dreams. The collected works of Ruthie Ruth sat waiting for lighter fluid and matches that Mz. El had waiting.

"I don't understand," said Ruthie. As she tried to retrieve the boxes, Mz. El refused her with a fiery pronouncement pushing her away, "Burn them. That's all they're good for."

Even Giv bared his teeth and barked and snapped at Mz. El and had to be restrained by Ruthie.

The old woman understood too well. Giv would protect the child against anyone, against all the absolutes of the universe if necessary. She was the meaning of his days, because he was explicitly love. He would stand as guardian, friend, compatriot and soldier till he fell.

Ruthie was shaken, "I don't understand."

"Do you know why there are schools?" said the old woman.

"Why there are—?"

Mz. El was of that generation that wanted answers to their questions now. "Do you know why?"

Confused, Ruthie answered, "So we can learn?"

"No. That is the end result. Do you know why there are schools, universities, libraries, museums?"

"No."

"Schools, universities, libraries, museums are the means by which to pass on knowledge and beauty. 'I now quote my betters,'" she said. "Knowledge and beauty are the measureless dreams of the soul. They are the origins of all."

Mz. El took Ruthie close to her and touched near to her heart where was inked, BE THE MIRACLE—"'Schools, universities, libraries and museums are a collection of miracles. Like you. Like what is there.'" She pointed to the boxes ready for the flame. "Those are the miracles in you. Just as there were miracles in Edison . . . as Louie Armstrong and jazz were a miracle . . . as there was a miracle in Lincoln . . . and Walt Whitman . . . and Judy Garland singing "Somewhere Over The Rainbow" and Edgar Allen Poe . . . and so with every living creature who poured out their beings . . . who revealed their souls to contempt or praise . . . to the last of themselves."

Mz. El again held out lighter fluid and match. She duly noted a perfectly realized flash of anger in the girl's eyes.

"I could, you know," said Ruthie.

"Yes, there's nothing like being dramatically and totally self-destructive, is there?"

⁓

IN LIEU OF A BURNING, Ruthie consigned herself to the creative. She got a part-time job in a tattoo parlor on Frenchman's Street, where she not only could bring Giv, but where the place was mercifully off tourist row.

She transformed her despair into drawings, her emotional pain into purity of purpose, her mortal condition to the limitless satisfaction of what mind and soul have to offer. Two boxes of art became three, then grew to four with sketches for fleshed-out stories. There were even ideas for children's books. One was to be a series born of the relationship between Bullet the cat and Giv. Of course, only in human terms could what they had be termed a "relationship." It would be more correctly described as a series of small tortures.

Bullet seemed convinced his life was dedicated to making Giv's miserable. He would disturb the dog's sleep with a swiftly passing swipe; he would steal Giv's food and use all his catly advantages in a personal war. The top of the breakfront and the space beneath the bureau in Ruthie's room were his main defensive fortifications.

Yet, one day, Giv got hold of Bullet's most prized

possession—a grey cloth mouse that made a squealy noise when teeth were sunk into it.

Right there in the living room with Bullet in a furious but helpless rage, Giv ate the mouse. Giv took a slow and loving revenge. Tail and legs disappeared into his mouth with spaghetti-like efficiency. The head made a most crunchy appetizer, and the body, a delightful main course that gave one last squealy cry as it was swallowed whole. Giv even licked his muzzle heartily when all was done. Then, to add insult to injury, he used his head to bam open the screen door and went for a snooze where the sun had snuck along the porch.

Of course, this only heightened antagonisms. Bullet would now lie in wait and leap from some high place onto Giv's unsuspecting back. Strike and run was his motto.

Ruthie watched and drew, as life and art melded, with Giv as the centerpiece. That was until the woman who cared for Bullet returned from her vacation.

"How was he?" she asked.

Mz. El, old school professional that she was, having learned the art of diplomacy while dealing with generations of parents, said quite cordially, "He's the worst S.O.B. I've ever been around. Other than that, he's a charm."

Then the tale of Bullet and the dog took a profound turn that would not only affect the little book Ruthie was creating, but life itself.

Bullet showed up one day at the screen door trying to get Giv's attention. Giv would come close but, after all, better to be on the inside, with your torturer on the outs. Day after day Bullet returned, and for long hours the two sat facing each other. At first Bullet did the usual hissing, but that mercurial attitude proved ineffective, and so the hissing began to subside, and eventually he took to gently scratching upon the screen.

Bullet, in a word, was lonely, and for all his faults, in dire need of friendship. He would slip home each day at twilight down through front yards, a solitary and sorrowful figure of a cat.

What Ruthie had been witness to wove her a whole new perspective on the story. She would add herself to it. In the book she would be a young girl drawing out the tale she was witnessing, a young girl who had recently lost a friend and was in dire need. Through the cat and the dog, this young imaginary Ruth would come to terms with that loss.

So, one day Ruthie opened the screen door and hoped for the best.

Possibility is a powerful ally, as are simplicity and goodness. And when she walked with Giv to Lake Pontchartrain the cat would stride along, his shiny eyes all protective and wary, and when Ruthie worked at her attic desk, the cat could often find an open window and sleek up the steps to find a place to sleep on the bed beside Giv. Of course, he was still an S.O.B., but he now reserved that attitude for strangers.

12

THE FLOOD

OOK AT THE cake, all lit up so that night with
candles, yet as they celebrated Ruthie's birthday
Governor Blanco declared a State of Emergency
in Louisiana as a hurricane named Katrina approached
landfall. Ruthie was nineteen that day, and in the birthday
card that Mz. El gave her she wrote: YOU ARE GROWING
LOVELIER BY THE HOUR.

The next day Katrina was upgraded to a Category 3.
Between nightfall and dawn it went from a Category 4
to a Category 5. Mz. El had never endured such rain. It
lashed against roof and walls like an ocean, a violent and
overwhelming ocean.

The women stayed together in the living room. Mz. El
on the couch, Ruthie in the big chair. Giv took to pacing
or moving from room to room. Ruthie had never seen

him so anxious. Then the lights flickered, they flickered and they surged, and then they failed.

Rafer came over the next morning. The streets were littered with branches and fallen trees. Another wave of rain came so hard it sounded like endless train wheels. He told his mother the news was reporting if Katrina pushed past Crescent City the levees might not hold. Mz. El's house was only a few blocks from the 17th Street Canal, and Katrina would reach Crescent City within hours.

Plans had to be made; contingencies for survival thought out. So, while the President was doing down-time and being duly warned the levees might well fail and decisive action was absolutely necessary, Ruthie and Mz. El were laboring like every other resident to save themselves. They were carting articles of importance, cherished mementos and valuables up to the attic. Ruthie took each box of drawings and put them in a plastic lawn bag, which she bound up tightly. Then she put that inside another lawn bag to secure it even more.

While the President shared a birthday cake photo-op with Senator John McCain, the 17th Street Canal was breached. Water hemorrhaged into the parish. You could hear it waterfall blocks away, seeking out every street and alley.

Ruthie had just left Rafer's house after loading all his boxed personals into her Volks. She and Giv were just turning past the park when the first surge of flooding gushed up under the chassis and through the wheel wells.

While the President promoted his Drug Care Benefit Program at a resort in Arizona, Ruthie and Mz. El were desperately trying to unload the car. Ruthie had driven right up onto the lawn so the Volks was by the porch steps. The water was up to Giv's haunches and there were fires. Great plumes of smoke began to infect the sky over Lake Pontchartrain.

While the President spoke in sunny California at a Senior Citizen Center about Social Security, the water began to top Mz. El's porch. It would not be long before they would have to retreat to the second floor and if necessary wait to be evacuated.

Mz. El looked in sorrow over her beloved neighborhood that was now a deepening lake. There was panic all along the block. People shouted to each other from house to house. An old man Mz. El had known since she was first married sat in his second story window and wept. Alarm systems failed everywhere. You could hear them down endless blocks.

"Mr. President, we need your help. We need everything you've got." The President went to sleep that night without acting on the Governor's request. And while he slept, a disaster of biblical proportions was turning a cherished part of American history into a wasteland.

The first floor of Mz. El's house had to be abandoned. She sat with Ruthie and Giv in the dark at the top of the stairwell. Whenever they heard what sounded like a rescue chopper or boat they turned up their flashlights and called out. Ruthie would go down and slog through the chest-high waters. The furniture in the living room looked like little more than tops of shipwrecked shadows.

She stood at the door. My God, the neighborhood. It was a moonlit deluge, dark and mourning and getting worse. Water leaked through half-sunk windows and the park . . . It had disappeared altogether.

She had gone downstairs a dozen times already, only to find nothing, but finally, a searchlight on a rescue boat seen was panning from house to house.

Ruthie yelled, "It's Rafer."

"Thank God," said Mz. El.

He already had two people in the boat. To hold it still was no easy task. Rafer helped his mother from the house through the worsening current. Ruthie held a duffel with extra clothes over her head so they wouldn't get wet. Giv had to leap and then swim to stay with them.

The woman next door shouted from a second-story window. Rafer and Ruthie got her from the house. All the way to the boat she kept asking, "Do you know where Bullet is . . . You haven't seen him? Are you sure?"

"He's not in the house?"

"I looked everywhere . . . What about your house?"

The woman was in a state of panic and wouldn't get in the boat without searching Ruthie's house. The current, of course, was worsening, and to hold that long for a search would be too long, especially with people so exhausted and soaked.

Rafer physically began to force her into the boat and she was crying and then Ruthie stopped him. "You're gonna come back, right?"

She grabbed a flashlight and was starting for the house before Rafer said, "No . . . get in the boat."

She was well out of reach, "You're coming back?"

Mz. El was calling to her.

"I've got to get everyone over the bridge where it's still dry. Then I'll come back. Two hours at the most."

"Take care of Giv!"

No sooner had she said it than Giv leapt from the boat. She ordered him back but he splashed and swam his way toward her.

⁓

HER FIRST INSTINCT was to search the attic. She called to Bullet as she ran the light over all his usual haunts, but there were so many boxes in her room. He could be anywhere, if he were here at all.

Suddenly she realized Giv was not with her. She felt a wave of distress and ran back downstairs calling to him. She saw him lying on the floor, his nose pinching into the space beneath the closed door to Mz. El's room.

She found the cat balled up and soaking wet beneath the old woman's bed. He lay there with the light right on him and no amount of coaxing could get Bullet to move. Ruthie had to crawl under the bed and ease that trembling body toward her.

All she said to him was, "If Mz. El ever knew you were in her room, under her bed . . ."

She dried the cat and then took up to watching from a front bedroom window. The cat lay beside Giv on the floor. An hour passed, then two. Rescue choppers crisscrossed the sky. One poured its light down somewhere up around Hammond Highway, though that seemed now like some great sunken expanse.

Ruthie grew frightened and sat on the floor with Giv. She tried to have a quiet dialogue with the night to calm herself. She rested against Giv's shoulder, fell in with his breathing. Yet the fear remained and grew more pronounced until it became a fathomable dread. As she lay there trying to weather that emotion, another came over her that Ian was there. It was mysterious and profound, and a sense of calm began to completely absorb her physical world.

Soon after, out of the void, she thought she felt the house move. She stood, uncertain. Giv sat and growled. Bullet began to nervously cry. She picked him up in her arms as Giv took off out the bedroom door. Wood was scraping wood somewhere.

She put the flashlight to the narrow hallway. Water had begun to seep along the floor. It glistened under that shiny beam. The stairwell no longer existed; it was now a well.

Again, she felt as if the house moved. She ran the light along the walls and ceiling. She held the beam on a light fixture. Its fluted glass was tremoring. She stepped close, it was quivering so in the bore of the flashlight. Why—

It hit the house like a battering ram. This monstrosity of trunk and branch powered by the current. Fifty feet of pure weight and force tore through the wall, blew out the hallway window, rained glass everywhere, scored the ceiling as it rose up into the rafters then came down upon the stairwell taking out part of the floor around it.

Ruthie did not feel a thing. The cat was thrown against the wall with a muted cry. The force of the trunk drove Giv back down the hall on his flanks. And the flashlight . . . it had come out of Ruthie's hand and was sinking into the dark waters around the stairwell where the floor had given way, turning slowly upon itself and sending up a long but momentary stile of light upon Ruthie's motionless body.

She floated there as one would stranded in the deep eons of night. Giv crawled around that rootless hull to find Ruthie floating and still where the edge of the floor had come undone. He put out a paw and touched her, but there was no response. Just pale breaths rising slowly through the black floodwater.

⌒

IT TOOK RAFER nearly another hour to return. When the rescue boat got near enough he called out to Ruthie but there was no response. He put the searchlight to the second-story windows. They looked back at him in helpless quiet. He had another officer with him this trip who anchored the boat by holding to a sill while Rafer climbed through the window.

Rafer moved through an inch of water. From the bedroom doorway he heard a gruff low metronomic pulling he could not quite make out. He put his searchlight to the hall. Details formed in a misty twilight. He had to look again to be sure. A tree had shattered a pathway through the back wall of the house to the stairwell. He called to Ruthie again, but there was only his voice coming back at him as a watery echo and that other sound, a low gruff metronomic huff that grew more clear and grittier as he approached.

He made his way carefully over that scored trunk, and that's when he saw them. They lay in a clump by the stairwell in an inch of water. Bullet was alive and clinging to Giv's back. Giv had managed somehow to pull Ruthie's body most of the way out of that black sump. The sound Rafer heard was Giv breathing through his nose for he still clasped Ruthie's shirt in his teeth. The muscles from his skull down through the withers were absolutely taut.

Rafer kneeled down and lifted Ruthie the rest of the way out of that stairwell with Giv still holding on. His searchlight cast upon the mark of her fatal wound. Rafer felt the world close down around him as he took her empty hand. He tried to have Giv let go, but Giv would not.

Rafer then tried to ease open Giv's jaw, but lost. He tried to force and pry it open, but was outwilled. Giv had lifted and pulled and held his Ruthie for at least an hour, probably as much as two. He would hold her yet. He would hold, if needed, until he fell.

So, while a President sleeps, a child of the nation passed away in a silent house on a flooded street in a great American city. She joined the ranks of those before her. This voice for good and beauty, this voice with endless futures, waiting to be discovered.

"Be the Miracle"—she and the meaning of the words were now bound together for eternity as one. She had lived out life's two great precepts—Love Thy Neighbor and I Am My Brother's Keeper. That is why a young girl with everything to live for went back into a black and flooding house to find a lowly cat.

When Mz. El wrote Ruthie's parents she quoted from a sermon by the Reverend at the church she had attended as a girl. He would handwrite the sermons on onion paper and pass them to each parishioner.

"The earth is the root of one tree and every living creature a lofty branch taking in the Holy Sun. While branches fall away to become lonely cemeteries with soundless bones, death is nothing, child, nothing. It is purely a means of removing the bark from our soul in preparation for the simples of eternity."

"And of this world, child, be at ease. You will not be forgotten. Goodness never is, nor beauty. The soul of you will be discovered. For a stranger will come out of the wilderness to see it happen. The stranger will prepare, as all must, for such a journey by being the most human of miracles."

Two years later

The Marine

13

WRITTEN IN BLOOD

S EE THE DOG. *He is a grey-looking thing with an arrow-shaped head. Just some nameless breed, come to us down through centuries of nameless breeds. But there he is, herding a flock of sheep along the Euphrates, all by his lonesome.*

This is where the original Adam was allegedly set up with the whole deal. Just keep it together, baby, and you won't have to work, or suffer, or die. It will be a steady stream of good times and chuckles. You know the rest. On that day the banks of the river Euphrates had less in common with the original creation than in a little creation of Dante's.

There is one image of the war that took place that day along the Euphrates that never leaves Sergeant Hickok, late of the U.S. Marines. It stays with him as what he describes in his journals as the timeless and frightening instant where the gifts of valor and the politics of insanity consume each other.

Sergeant Dean Hickok, all of twenty-four, had managed to crawl away from his overturned Humvee. He had dragged an unconscious platoon mate with him. The Humvee was being consumed by flames. He leaned back against a concrete stanchion and took up a defensive position to protect what was left of his patrol.

He was by a bridge over the Euphrates. A piece of metal rodding near a foot long speared his side when the Humvee took an RPG. The metal rodding still protruded from beneath his ribcage, and the Sergeant, staring down at the wound as he chambered his fifty-caliber said, "I look like a f——n' hors d'oeuvres." Then he saw a pickup racing over this bridge and bearing down on him.

The firefight had escalated. One of the Sergeant's platoon mates lay nearby and screamed incoherently. Hickok himself was bleeding to death while he fired away at the pickup trying to make its way across the bridge. The expended shells from his fifty-caliber were like a metallic hailstorm on the concrete he leaned against. He was cut over one eye by a shell casing and the blood nearly blinded him.

All the while, there was this dog . . . this raggedy-haired, underfed, son of a nameless breed, calm and steady, shepherding his flock through a godforsaken wasteland of garbage and war-torn refuse.

For a few more seconds there was a burning fusillade from the Sergeant's fifty-caliber as he bore down on the pickup. Then there was an explosion and pieces of the truck rained down on the grey dead Euphrates.

The Sergeant tried to fashion a few words to his other platoon mate, the one that was screaming incoherently, but to what purpose? He wanted desperately to help him, to reach him, but the rod through his side as he tried to move was a hideous reminder of how badly he was wounded.

Hickok fought to remain conscious by shouting down the pain, by calling it out with every vile and kinked-out epithet he could come up with. He had wounded soldiers to protect, and a position to defend. He wiped the blood from his eyes. That dog, look at him. Firefight or no firefight. He yelled to the dog, as if he could really even hear or know, "You doin' all right, man? You doin'—?"

The Sergeant slumped over. He was now staring up at a cloudless flat sky, the indifferent and hot concrete against his back. Then he was just falling away, like a meteorite through blind stellar depths.

FOR SOME, the hardest part of being in any war is surviving it. This was Sergeant Hickok. Two of his squad had died, including the interpreter. One had lost a leg. Another was lying up in Walter Reed with permanent brain damage that left him talking incoherently. Hickok lost a kidney, as the metal rod had skewered it.

He was awarded the Purple Heart and a Silver Star for bravery under fire. Every time he looked at the medals, all he did was cry. It got so he could not look at them at all, as they represented the maimed and dead close to him he could not save. What was the old Bob Dylan line, ". . . either I'm too sensitive, or else I'm getting soft."

Like so many Americans of good faith, he had signed up after 9/11. He had been at Syracuse University at the time studying journalism. To pay his way through school, he'd worked as a janitor at Upstate Medical Center. Dean had been on M Street having breakfast when the Towers were hit. The place packed up fast with shocked students. The dreadful one never imagined happening had happened.

Dean's older sister had worked in Tower Two. His calls to her cell went unanswered. The silence spoke volumes. The next day, Dean had been in New York carrying a photo and walking the hospitals.

No matter where you were in N.Y. those first days, you were downwind. Even birds on rooftops were coated with the ashes of the dead. He had searched everywhere; he was like a hand grasping through prison bars for the slightest hope.

The world at that moment was a few square blocks of sorrow. People were so kind, so giving; it was almost too much to bear. Even reporters in the street, in all their self-aggrandizement, could not help but be humbled under the siege of such humanity.

Days later Hickok had received word some of his sister's remains were at a makeshift morgue in Jersey. Some remains . . . to hear it said like that . . . uttered in undertones.

He was now utterly and profoundly alone. All that was left was a two-family home in Flushing, by the old '64

World's Fair site. This is where his sister had lived. There had been a statue of St. Francis of Assisi in the backyard. He and his sister had posed beside it for how many birthdays?

He had gone and sat on the front porch one last time. The neighborhood had changed, much as the nation had changed. Language had grown coarser, dreams more grainy, attitudes more uncivil.

He'd enlisted the next day.

Sergeant Hickok had been there when the statue of Saddam was taken down, and the world watched on the news. He felt a trace of the heavens in his throat as it fell. *This is for my sister; this is for those who died on 9/11; this is for all Americans, for all people who have suffered an atrocity.* If victory were as easy as creating a ruin, then God would be inconsequential. The design of immortal intelligence proves that over and over again.

SEE THE DOG. He is caged and starving to death in a shed. He has been left without even water. He is getting to the point where a pitiful sigh demands great physical effort. But Giv does not intend to die that easily. His eyes may have become hollows and his body like the protruding ribcage of a crucified Christ, but there is within him an innate will to survive.

There is no written record of Giv's life from the day when Mz. El was lost to him, and he ended up in that cage in a shed in Bullitt County, Kentucky, where animals were kept hidden then sold off to be used in experiments.

I will call these years, for now, the lost years. As I said, there is no written record, but there is a record. Oh, yes.

It will become known in time and not long after this tale is done. As a matter of fact, it will be because of this tale that those years become known.

Giv was not alone in that shed tucked back in the Kentucky woods. There were other cages with other dogs. Some had already succumbed. One howled plaintively, but no one heard.

Inside Giv, he understood. The order of endless dawns passed down from generation to generation lived inside him. If he could not free himself, he would die. He had been close to death before, and he knew he was close again.

He could also smell the night beyond those shed doors and it smelled of cool summer thunderheads being carried on the wind. There were thin flashes of momentary white to be seen through a slight hole in the shed roof. The night air spoke of rain, and rain spoke of hope.

Rain. It would fall from the sky. It would drip from branches and runnel down the trunk of trees. It would collect in boot tracks, and rabbit tracks. It would form meager soppy puddles. But would it be enough, enough to cool his dried-out mouth and throat, enough to keep the weakened flesh going? It could save your life, if only . . .

The rain began in a slow and steady metronome on the shed's tin roof. The cadence of its quiet call straight from the center of heaven. Every beast, including man, ever blessed with life knew what rain portended. Its poetry was so absolutely human and life affirming.

Reach the rain. You have to free yourself from this prison you were placed in by human oppressors to whom you are nothing more than pocket money.

You were not created for this. You are a child of limitless love that existed before man. Even though you are touched by injury and pain, you are not forgotten, or helpless. You are a soul with a destiny wrapped in human warmth even when you are treated as something worthless. Remember, you are not without worldly friends who mean to see you well.

Giv had one choice—escape. The only way to escape was to eat through the crate that imprisoned him. The only opening was this thin space between the plastic framing and grated metal door. But there was nothing he could sink his teeth into, so he was left with one thin possibility. To open his jaws wide and use his teeth as knives to score the plastic near the grated opening.

He did this again and again, feverishly, until his neck sinew and breath were expended, and when expended, when he had nothing to show for his effort except furrows dug into the resilient plastic, and his tongue was dry and coarse and cut, and his paws had proved useless clawing at the crate wall, Giv stopped. His head dropped in exhaustion.

The rain. It was dripping through an unfixed hole in the roof. There was a pulse to it that countered the grave silence and a dog howling.

And in that moment you wonder, do they know? You wonder, was Anna Perenna there at that moment inside him whispering to go on? Was his father there? Angel, Ruthie Ruth, Mz. El? Was it just immediate pure energy or the invisible hand of the world at work?

His mouth opened again and he began to press as hard as he could, scoring the plastic with his teeth in the exact spot that was wet with his bloody saliva.

The noise it made was like a nail cutting across concrete. You could hear it outside the shed. You could hear it above the rain and along the river path with its dark loomwork of brush; you could hear far back in the bowers of that pine forest where the shed was hidden from the world; you could hear it along the old logging road where people now clandestinely came to dump their garbage and deface nature.

Then there was a noise unlike the others. A tooth had cut through. It hooked up there and Giv anchored his jaw and twisted his head so it was flat against the crate wall, and then he jerked it around and the plastic snapped.

There was a thimble-sized hole now, with spider cracks around it. The rain on the tin roof was coming down hard and heavy and the world of the shed was shrouded in it. But it was the scent of the rain, so close and rich with life.

Giv bore down on the plastic. He could get one tooth and part of another all the way through. His breath came out in deep huffs and he pulled together all his strength and attacked again. His muzzle ratcheted so violently the crate tipped over on its side, but another piece of plastic had given way.

He could slip his tongue all the way through now. The sharp crate edges cut the flesh. He pushed it out into the dark. He could feel the night air on a slight breeze through the crooked shed door.

But it was the rain. Those first few drops dripping from the rafters by that unfixed stretch of shed roof. The hollow eyes were fixed now. The other dogs were growing excited by the ferocious noise and the smell of blood. Giv could bite into a mouthful of plastic. Each piece he tore off gashed the flesh around his muzzle.

He could force his muzzle through the hole and the long thin, spidery cracks that branched from the opening started to flower outward as he pushed. He could feel free air in his nostrils.

He went to pull his head back so his teeth could bear down against the crate wall, but as he did, the jagged edges that had flowered outward receded back and formed a sharply pointed noose around his neck.

He panicked. He tried to free his head turning it side to side, but all he did was manage to cut himself down one ear. His body froze. His legs shook.

With every breath he took, the crate wall around his head seemed to breathe with him. It was like a living thing there in the darkness. A creature meaning to hold fast.

There was no going back. The pain was equal either way. So Giv just leaned forward precariously with his head and pushed. You could hear the plastic try to resist, but he pushed and made headway. Then he took one paw and lifted it. There was just enough room, just enough to wedge it between his head and the crate edges, but they cut into the flesh. Screed it horribly. In a surge another piece of plastic cracked off and the leg was free.

But the weight of the leg and his head dangling wildly outside the crate caused it to topple over again, and there was Giv with his muzzle flat against the raw earth and this cage humped up on his back.

The rain. It was collecting on the shed floor and creating tiny rivulets where the ground sloped. There was one just a lick from his nose. He lay there and lapped at the viscous paste till his tongue was black and gritty.

But his insides—the water was like a touch of fire reaching that secret place inside the body that fuels the will. He tried to move his pelvis and get the weight off his one free leg. Using that, and with the side of his head pressed into the ground, Giv began to muscle himself upright. He tottered and fell, but rose again. He poured all his strength into that one free leg, and it held this time at a cockeyed angle.

Then he started for the shed door. He stumped along with one free leg like some bizarre drunk dragging this edifice that was cocooned around the rest of his body.

He hobbled and slipped and hobbled across that muddy shed floor, with its beer bottles and food wrappers and ground-out cigarettes. Foot by suffering foot over earth that stunk of abuse.

But those shed doors were getting closer, strips of rainy night slipped through the slightly open, rotted frames.

The shed doors were chained closed but not so closed he couldn't wriggle himself through the opening if he rid himself of that imprisoning crate. He leaned against one door, as the leg carrying him was near collapse. He poked his muzzle out and the chains rattled and the door moved slightly.

The rain streaked down his face and over his eyes and into his mouth. And these were not the silty licks he'd had to lap from the earth. This rain was from the headwaters of Time. This was the water of baptisms and miracles. If only he could see the telling beauty of resolve defined on his dripping, wet face.

He dragged himself, head stretched out like a divining rod through that spare opening but the crate locked up. The doors formed the dark physical geography of a wedge that he could not phalanx through.

14

SAVED

EE THE DOG. *He is being drenched with rain as he tries to pull himself free using the doors as braces. Like the butterfly out of the cocoon, the bird out of the egg, the child from the womb—yet what he is trying to free himself of is a greedy human dream exacted by man to whom heartbreak is less than pocket change.*

Can you hear the crate begin to groan, the plastic continue to crack? Imagine if you could anchor two good legs in that runny mud.

Yes, your flesh was being bared. Yes, a rib was being broken. Yes, your jaw was in seizure as you cried out the pain. But the crate could not hold. It was giving way, in a series of nasty, weakening snaps. This prison was not as strong as the will granted you when the first giver breathed life into the black void.

And there in the moonless rain, by a river path near a forgotten logging road, without either witness or friend, Giv freed himself.

SOMEWHERE OUTSIDE D.C., heading west over the Appalachians, Dean turned off the main highway.

Main highways are for people who have destinations, with appointments to keep, schedules to maintain, urgencies to deal with or dreams awaiting. Dean was none of these.

He wore the look of a nearly broken soul as he crossed the blue paling mountains. Any lesser road, any backwater two-lane blacktop where the night emptiness would wash the visage of Washington out of his mind, would do.

He had just been to Walter Reed to see one of his platoon mates and share sorrow with the family.

Private H. Hughes had been nicknamed "The Hunk" for obvious reasons. He was now confined to a bed with permanent brain damage. Pieces of shrapnel from the RPG that had taken out their Humvee had seared through parts of his skull and left them little more than wet bread.

The Hunk was hooked up to catheters and IV's and a battery of machines and monitors. He lay there in that sterile eight-by-ten with the sun white-hot on the far wall like some beautiful Frankenstein with eyes that buoyed in their sockets lifelessly until there was a seizure. Then they would roll back into his head, and those beautiful blue pupils that had turned women into little puddles of pure infatuation became these fluttering repositories of veined white—pathetic and frightening at the same time. The chest and legs would stiffen, the hands begin to jerk at the wrist. And while his parents would wait for the nurses, they would try to cradle and soothe their most precious son. They would whisper to this once powerful figure of youth in whom they had poured all their hopes and dreams, as if he were still that child who could hear and understand.

And if this were not painful enough, he would begin to talk. He would become in a coherent, yet incoherent, way Private Hughes again, and he was on patrol. He was somewhere along the Euphrates riding in that Humvee and serving his nation. Being the good, proud footsoldier, serving the flag of our fathers in all that dust and smoke. Ever vigilant, even in a living death. The Purple Heart he had been awarded hung from his bed, to be seen by all.

"The last full measure"—Lincoln's words. That was all Dean had thought of as he watched his squad mate and friend, and those suffering parents who would now live the endless battle until the battle ended.

The three had stood out in the daylight before Dean left. If ever death was cloaked in silence, that was it. He had been desperate not to cry in front of them. Not because he was afraid of showing vulnerability, but as a matter of respect for a friend and especially those parents. They were owed the grace of strength. To Dean they were not just the boy's parents, they were every parent who had been bled by the words, "the last full measure."

Before Dean left the room he had leaned down and whispered to his friend, near silently, "If only I could have done more." Then Dean went to attention and saluted a young man he had shared filth and blood and dreams with.

The thought he'd failed had him. There is only one way to navigate such alleged internal failure, and that is through human limits. Limits that define the true expanse of man. To understand that you are not all, but only a part of all. It means coming to terms with one's human limitations to exact an outcome, and then being able to be at one with the outcome. There are shadows that pass over all our lives, and you must embrace them as you would embrace anyone you ever loved.

Realize that these shadows, these failures, these limits, are guidelines to human capacity, and they will guide you to an ever-expanding state of being—if you accept them.

This is an essential to the gospel of life on earth. But Dean Hickok, Sergeant Hickok late of the U.S. Marines, as he made his way into Kentucky, was not ready for that kind of acceptance. He had too much self-destructive rage.

He crossed the state amidst revelations of rain and his complete disconnect to the war. What had started in Iraq with such honorable intentions had melted before his eyes. The minds behind the undertaking had proved to be utterly unprepared, and in their mediocrity they had proved that being unprepared was not an accident but a continual state of being.

Would the wounded and dead—from the Twin Towers and the Pentagon and Flight 93, to the desert firestorm that began with shock-and-awe—never sleep the sleep of the honorably vindicated? Would they be left forever an unfinished tragedy? Would the "last full measure" of their being end as another footnote in our nation's history of misjudgment as to where the real enemy resides?

Dean drank that night at a roadside bar called "Three Women." A hipster photograph of the lady owners dressed as the Fates took up one cinderblock wall. It was a nice touch of self promotion.

Next thing, he had begun to cry. These three women doing the Fates routine were about the same age as his lost sister. She had never been in a hurry to go anywhere; rather she'd found satisfaction and happiness being just where she was. And of all the things about her, what he could not get out of his mind, was the end. Had she suffered? Had she died in terror? Did she choke to death in the smoke? Had she come face-to-face with finality? The business of darkness is bad business.

Luckily he had taken up in a lonely corner booth. He kept his head down and somewhat covered. *What a mug shot I would make*, he thought. At that moment there were no bandages for the gallery of spears he felt going through him, and when he finally heard himself sob and looked up and noticed someone at the bar turning in his direction, he quickly left.

He drove from where the rain began to where it grew

much worse. His throat hurt from ruthless crying and somewhere on a strip of road in Bullitt County, Kentucky, he wished the cruelest wish of all—that his life would end.

The one near impossible habit for man to break is his ability to play the worst tricks of all upon himself. When the mind becomes thine enemy, the death card is one of its tricks.

Dean turned a profile to his better instincts and pressed the gas pedal. The dark world of the woods passed in silence, faster and faster. The rain-swept road was all black and sinister and he turned the volume on the radio way up.

There is nothing like dying to music. Movies have made a living out of it. Even in Iraq, soldiers had crowded their heads with high-octane chords and riffs and punched-up lyrics to get battle ready.

But somewhere before an irresistible desire became an irrevocable decision, Dean Hickok, late of the U.S. Marines, spotted something on the road.

SEE THE DOG—through streams of rain across the windshield and down a long tunnel of smoky headlights crumpled up on its front paws as the car bore down on him.

The flesh around Dean's throat tightened. Something came out of his mouth that sounded like "no." He spun the wheel. At the speed he was going, Dean was beyond the limits of the tires. His face drained of all that had been on his mind. He was leaving a threadline of burning rubber as he hit the brakes. The dog tried to move but his spindle-shanked body could only rise up partly and totter a foot or so.

Dean kept pulling the wheel hard. The car was now out of control. He was going at breakneck speed right into a disaster, off the road and onto the shoulder, which dropped away.

The car hit a post of some kind and Dean's head rammed against the driver's window, and like that he was blind as a stone in the dark and everything sounded far away and he pressed down on the brakes again, but it was useless. He ducked but he didn't know why exactly except the car seemed to be listing to one side. He could hear metal getting raked and then there was this other sound like that day along the Euphrates in the Humvee. Glass and metal melding into one hurtling shriek.

His body was moving like a marionette. Everything in slow motion as if he were without shape or weight in the dark void of some dream. Then all was still. All was silent. He was not there, and then maybe he was. His fingers seemed to be the first of him to sense and feel. He started to put together the pieces of what he saw around him. The radio was still playing, and a smoky haze floated above the hood.

He could see himself reflected in the windshield. There was blood running down his face. He looked like he took ten rounds' worth of beating from a heavyweight in all of ten seconds. The car was a wreckage wedged between two trees. If it wasn't for the seat belt he was wearing, he'd be sprawled somewhere out beyond the wreckage waiting to be bagged and drained.

He undid the seat belt. *Who goes to commit suicide wearing a seat belt anyway? What the f—k was I thinking?* Just the notion of it now seemed a lifetime ago.

He was surprised to find he could move. He was more surprised to find he could stand. He hovered there by the car. Everything seemed thin and far away. It took time but he managed to finally struggle up to the shore of the road.

The dog . . .

Dean looked about. There it was, near exactly at the spot he'd last seen it, still crumpled down on its front paws.

He made his way toward the animal fighting a dizziness that meant to sweep him from his feet. He wiped at the blood on his face, feeling the long gash where it came from above one eye.

He stood over the hobbled creature. He could not believe what he saw. If ever there was a picture of the pitiful, this was it. The dog looked to be something made from graveyard parts. Its coat was manged, there were cuts and tears along the flesh and festery welts across its back.

Dean kneeled down beside the dog and its head came up to face him. Dean put out a hand. "I'm not going to hurt you," he said, but the dog's muzzle recoiled.

He made no further attempt. Rather he just remained like so talking to the animal and looking up and down in the darkness for any sign of a vehicle. "You can't stay here like this."

Dean moved his hand closer to the dog's muzzle. "If you're gonna bite me, you're gonna bite me. But I'm gonna give you a handful . . ."

He tried to be as soothing as an old familiar, and he held his shaky hand out in peace so the dog could smell it and get comfortable, but the dog's eyes didn't seem to be able to focus. He was either groggy or in some state of shock. He didn't have a collar so Dean eased his hand down on the back of the dog's neck, and his other hand he slipped under the breastbone to try and get him to stand. But as he did, a bleating sound came out of the dog, and his mouth hung open and the body bent toward the right. There was something, some wound.

The dog couldn't move or wouldn't move, but he had to move, so Dean treated him like any wounded soldier. He braced his arms under that dog's emaciated body and lifted. The dog winced again, and his legs hung there limp.

There they were in the Kentucky rain. Two veterans of wars and prisons, and all manner of sorrows and meaningless violence. A shadow with a shadow struggling to the shoulder, leaving droplets of blood behind them.

Dean managed to get the dog to the car. He lay him on the backseat carefully. He then grabbed his army coat from the floor and covered the poor beast with it.

He looked for his cell, which had been on the dashboard but was now nowhere to be found. He came out of the car cursing and wiping at the blood on his face, when he saw far, far down the road two islands of light streaming through the pines.

He expended the energy he had left running up that hill and backsliding more than once in all that runny muck. The grey smoky light was coming on fast. He could see it against pine bowers and a black sky.

The accident was catching up to him. The smells, the exhaust and burnt rubber, the foul odors coming off that torn-up engine took him back to Iraq. The Iraq of car bombs going off in heat-filled streets with their knots of screaming wounded around the burnt-up dead. Human waste lying in human waste.

His body began to shudder all the way up from the bottom of his gut. A burning of ghastly bile swamped right up into his nose. He was on his knees when the light rushed along the rain-soaked asphalt and right up over him.

A van came to a skidding halt. There were kids in the van, a couple of years younger than himself. They were talking over each other as they scrambled around him.

"My car," he said and pointed toward where it had rammed through some fencing. One of the kids was already on a cell calling 911. Dean put a hand on another's shoulder, "In my car . . ." He was starting to pass out. "My . . . there's a dog."

15

TWO VETERANS

"**S**EE HIM. See him. Take a real look."

Dean was in an emergency room when he regained consciousness. His wound was being treated and stitched. He was told by a nurse to lie still. He couldn't see much but he could hear this woman's voice, frustrated and angry somewhere nearby. "I want you to look at the pictures and see the dog. See what was done to it. Feel what was done to it."

Dean moved his head a bit toward the voice even though he was being told to lie still. He could see through a gap between the curtains two policemen talking with a woman in medical greens with her hair pulled back. It seemed she worked at a local animal hospital and had been sent to pick up the dog. She had snapshots in her hand and was forcing one of the officers to look. "I want you to see what he did to the dog."

"I was there," said the officer, "I saw the dog."

The second officer was going through Dean's wallet and found the Purple Heart and Silver Star. He knew what they were right away having been in the brotherhood of boots. The officer tried to get his partner's attention to show him the medals, when Dean said, "Put them back."

Surprised, the officer turned.

"Did you hear me? Put them back."

Dean didn't care if he was being stitched. He brushed the doctor's hand away and sat up even as the nurse tried to keep him from doing so. He had to hold onto the sides of the gurney to keep from going over. "I said put them back." He was sitting there with thread and needle hanging from a half-stitched gash. "They have nothing to do with you."

The officer picked up something in Dean's voice he'd heard with other vets. It was living with an isolation and pain at having experienced a place that warrants such things as medals. You never want to see them again, but you keep them close to you. And for that same reason, no one should touch them or even have access to them. Because they are beyond symbols of courage or service. They are a sacred reminder of the price paid in human treasure.

The officer did as he was asked.

⌐

THEY FINISHED THE stitching while Dean sat there and explained coming upon the dog.

The woman by the curtain interrupted, "He's lying."

The officer waved her to be quiet.

Dean stared at her. "Slapping your face wouldn't be out of the question."

"Those kids," she said, "when they called animal emergency told me, *he* said it was his dog."

"I never said any such thing."

"They're just making it up?"

One of the officers pointed out, "It is what the kids said."

The woman mumbled, "Slapping your face wouldn't be out of the question."

"It's not my dog."

"How many times have you heard this story?" she said to everyone. "You stop a camper and find in the back a near-dead fighting dog, and they tell you we just found him on the road and were bringing him to a shelter. How many abused dogs do you find—?"

"Go wait in the hall, right now," said the officer who'd found Dean's medals.

The woman obeyed reluctantly, but before she did, she took one of the snapshots she'd had of the dog and flicked it at Dean. It landed on the gurney beside him. "Keep it as a memento to your manhood."

⁓

THE DOCTOR WANTED Dean to stay overnight for observation; Dean chose to quietly disappear the first chance he got. He came upon a motel a few blocks from the hospital.

One of those courtyard jobs where gaudy wallpaper and bedspreads with decades worth of fray are standard issue.

He had been advised not to drink with a concussion, but he bought a sixer of Budweiser anyway. He sat on the bed facing the bureau mirror and did a hard survey of himself.

His disheveled hair hung down over his forehead where he'd been bandaged. He looked beat, but that tight focus was coming back to those dark eyes. On his shoulder was a decal he'd gotten after basic: U.S. MARINE—ARE YOU READY TO RUMBLE.

He had come to a moment within himself that night. A hard-to-imagine place of the human soul that stole down upon him like a phantom. But it was no phantom. It was Sergeant Dean Hickok, late of the U.S. Marines.

On the bureau was the snapshot that had been thrown at him. He'd kept it, though he was not sure why. It had been taken at the animal hospital. Fluorescent light shined down on a stainless steel table where the dog lay. There was something about a wounded living thing lying on stark cold silver. Dean could understand why the woman was so angry. Daylight turned the reality of what he saw last night into a whole other reality. He felt bad for having said what he had to the woman.

THE NEXT MORNING he learned his car was a total. He finished off the Budweiser and walked a strip of used car lots. He found an SUV with four-wheel drive. The engine had been kicked up and the rig was pure grey primer. He bought it because it appealed to some renegade spirit.

He stopped at the impound lot to get his things. He meant to put this county behind him after one simple errand.

At the animal hospital he asked the attendant about the dog that was brought in last night from the accident. The bandage above the eye said pretty much who Dean was.

A few minutes later a vet came down the hallway from a room where they did surgeries. Dean could momentarily see a dog being operated on.

The vet was an older man. He scrutinized Dean carefully. "Is there something you want?"

Dean tried to explain how it wasn't his dog. But that he wanted to know was the dog all right, and could he give some money for its care?

The vet explained the dog suffered from malnutrition, severe dehydration, a broken rib, and there was something else. He took from his work-coat pocket a plastic baggie. Dean could see what looked to be pieces of flesh-colored plastic with jagged edges.

"These are parts of a crate. I took them from the dog's gums and mouth, from his neck, his chest, his legs. He must have eaten his way through it."

The way the vet held the plastic baggie and stared, Dean had this fleeting notion, that without saying it, the vet thought he was in some way culpable.

"Barring one of these shards cutting through his stomach

or intestines, he should survive. As for money . . . thank you, but no thank you."

On his way out, Dean stopped at the front desk and asked the attendant, "What's going to happen to the dog?"

"We'll try to find a rescue home. If not, he goes to the shelter. He could end up being put down."

⁓

HE WAS LEAVING Bullitt County behind, but as he gassed up, a disquieting urge came over him to go back to the site of the accident.

The place was near as lonely as the night before. But in daylight, under a purely beautiful sky with the perfume of vintage forest smells all about him, Dean felt this sense of oneness and wonderment with the world.

Then he stood by the fence he had torn through and looked into the decline where his car had left slashing marks in the earth till it scored the trees. *Why am I here?* he thought.

He looked at the spot on the road where the dog had been. And the journalist he had once-upon-a-time aspired to be asked a question. *Why was the dog here?*

The question was both practical and philosophical in nature.

He walked both shoulders of the road searching for clues. A broken rib, those wounds—he could not have come far. Had he been dumped somewhere here in a crate? Maybe. If so, where was the crate? Of course, he could have, say, been in the back of a truck and eaten his way out of the crate, then being discovered, he was dumped. Dean could see scenarios within scenarios.

Dean walked through the sloping brush and came to what had once been a logging road maybe fifty yards from where his SUV was parked.

He kept asking himself, *why am I here? Right here? Why is my life, my life? Am I just a Silver Star and a shamble of memories?*

He wanted to know, not unlike anyone else, if there were something that inscribed our existence upon the universe. Some said God was shrewd enough to never answer that question, leaving it to be a matter of faith. Of course, faith could be nothing more than the recurring banality of a thousand asides or it could take its place among the pantheons of belief.

Sergeant Dean Hickok, late of the U.S. Marines, a war hero and a most decent soul, had no faith. Had he ever? He couldn't say.

But there was a reason why that image in Iraq had never left him of that dog guiding those sheep, and weathering a safe course through a firefight. The animal had been practical, unwavering and brave.

Dean hadn't wandered very far. A few dozen yards maybe. He walked amidst the garbage dumped there. This would be a place to leave a dog in a crate, and so he searched.

Alongside the logging road was a creek. He walked through vine-strangled brush to its edge. If the dog had been free to drink, would he be dehydrated as the vet had said?

He flashed on that dog with the sheep. The shore of the

Euphrates where the firefight had taken place was much like this, lined with garbage. He could remember the dog with its razory head, by the hull of a bombed-out vehicle, as the sheep crowded up around him.

The sun was high and behind Dean. He could see his shadow there on the creek with all that clear water surging over it. He stood there dissolving into the image of that clear water on the creek surface passing over him when something disturbed the calm.

It was as much human as it was not. He angled his head to hear more closely. A sound.

There is one thing about having been in war. Your senses get attuned to the edges of sound, as that is where danger and threats lie in wait. There had been a rumor in his camp of a soldier stationed up in the Triangle of Death who could hear the rifle click of a sniper preparing to fire at a distance farther out than the sniper could fire.

There it was again, striking at the silence. That sound. A cry and howl all coiled together.

He had the sound in his crosshairs now. He was running toward it. The sound echoed as if coming from the inside of a coffin. And not far back in the dark light of the trees, he discovered the shed.

He could see and smell through the meager opening between those chained shed doors. He found a piece of bedframe beside a rotted mattress, and while he called the animal hospital on his cell he pried the door hinges from that rotting wood.

By the time a van arrived he had the cages out and in the light. He'd rummaged the garbage for anything that could hold water for a dog to drink from. Most were able to walk, and they lapped at the creek water till they choked. The others were too weak, or dead.

He helped get the dogs back to the hospital. He even brought along a gnawed-through crate he had found in the shed, which interestingly enough was near the same color plastic as the shards in that baggie.

Luckily a restaurant about a block from the animal hospital had a bar. Dean needed to drink away some of what he had seen. The woman from the night before came in and sat beside him. He learned that her name was Veronica.

"I'm sorry," she said. There was a humbled honesty to her that made Dean feel all too human.

"He ate his way through that crate," said Dean, "and struggled up there to the road. He had to tear himself out. I could see marks on the shed doors; it was all scarred from the crate where he tried to drag it through." Dean paused. "Did he understand he was dying? He must have. But he willed himself past it. He's got a lot of . . ." He was going to say "soldier in him" . . . but the word spoke of too much.

"The dog," said Veronica, "had a registration implant. You know, what they place under the skin for identification. His name is Giv . . . G-I-V. And he belongs with a woman named Ruthie Ruth. We tried to contact her but got nowhere. All the information we had was from New

Orleans just months before Katrina. It's been three years and who knows what else."

They sat a while and drank in the cool quiet of that afternoon bar.

When it was time for Veronica to get back to the hospital she offered to pay, but Dean wouldn't have it. As she got up she slipped some money into his t-shirt pocket anyway, then she touched his shoulder in a quiet, tender fashion.

"I'd like to ask you a favor," he said. "I'm traveling to California . . . Barrett Junction. I'm told it's north of San Diego. I have to pay my respects to the father of a platoon mate killed during a firefight we were in. I would take the dog and drive to New Orleans first and see if I can find this . . . whatever her name is."

Veronica, who was standing next to him, now sat back down. "Realistically, I don't think you'd have much luck."

"I would do it."

"And if you don't find her, what then?"

"I'll find him a good home. The man I'm going to see is a veteran. He lives in an area with a lot of vets from Iraq and the Gulf War. Let me share something with you."

There were outdoor runs at the back of the animal hospital. Long runs that were roofed but partly open to the sun. Giv was lying on his outstretched paws with the warmth shining down on him. But the light only deepened the shadows where his flesh fell away from the ribs.

Dean had seen the dog that morning after returning from the shed. Dean had talked a bit and the dog sat there stoically, then his head rose and cocked slightly to one side. It seemed to him when this dog was primed and fully fleshed, he would be a handsome and strong dog. There was also something else he'd noticed.

The eyes. They did not look away. They stared and they stared even when Dean stopped talking and just leaned against the gate to the run. And these were not the shocky eyes of the night before. They were more tightly focused and that made the dark in them, and of them, all the more formidable.

Dean related all this to Veronica as they sat at the bar.

"This is the favor," said Veronica. "Taking him."

"Yes."

"Why do you want to do this?"

Dean had been sitting there with his hands around his drink, which he stared at as he talked, and now his hands opened outwardly as if trying to grapple with certain feelings. "I see that dog on the road last night. I see that shed. I see him in the run today. I . . ." for a moment he was going to open up about where he was on that road last night, what he was feeling; instead he told her, "What does he have really . . . nothing."

She heard his voice slightly give way on the word "nothing."

"And that," he said, "is a state of being I truly know about."

16

DOWN THE MISSISSIPPI

*S*EE HIM *framed in the rearview mirror, lying in the back of the SUV heading west with Dean Hickok, late of the U.S. Marines.*

Dean had put the back seats down so Giv had plenty of stretch room. Giv lay with his head resting on a Marine duffel, which got his muzzle just high enough to take in the wind coming through the open windows.

Dean was loaded down with dog food and treats and vitamins and meds, even a jerry-rigged wooden ramp to drop over the back end of the SUV, as Giv, with his broken rib, couldn't jump in and out of the vehicle. The rig had been turned into a fast-moving-grey-primered-torqued-out-four-wheel-drive supply depot of dog essentials, with Dean as driver.

Before they'd left the hospital one of the attendants

had brought out an old but useable crate for the dog, on the chance Dean wanted one. It was near the same color as the crate he'd found in the shed. Giv had expended an awful lot of blood on that crate.

"No crate, thank you," was all Dean had said.

The trip across Illinois was pretty much inconsequential. They were just two strangers wearing their own personal brand of silence, but Dean wondered about what the dog had been through, beyond the crate. What had he suffered? It wasn't till they reached East St. Louis that he saw for himself.

Along the way Dean stopped a couple of times for the dog. Always at a remote place, a rest area or a stretch of country quietude. The dog didn't go far, not with those near-starved legs and broken rib. But Dean could see in the dog the first real brush with being free and able to just sit or get his nose into all that high grass.

In East St. Louis, it was a different story.

Dean pulled into a truck stop near the Mississippi River. It was that soft blue after sunset when the lights first go on and the earth begins to cool. Behind the truck stop was a long run of grass that led to a stand of trees. The great river was just beyond it.

Dean thought about walking all the way to the shore, but as traffic and dark were setting in, he brought a leash with a choke chain when he opened the back of the SUV to let Giv out.

Up to now he had not used a leash, there'd been no need. But when he got the dog out of the truck and was about to put that choke chain around his neck, Giv curled up and slunk down pulling his head away, and his eyes began to flutter and blink in fear. His whole countenance was a statement of submission and surrender, and he started trembling at Dean's slightest movement toward him.

Dean had no idea what was wrong and reached out with the hand that had the leash, which rattled like chain mail, and Giv recoiled completely, bending near in half his head bowed to the ground. He remained just so, at the humbled, horrid fringes of existence and shivering uncontrollably. It was the accumulated weeping of years expressed in that body; and those eyes that peered up at Dean nearly begging, yes, begging for pity to be spared inhuman and uncalled-for pain.

It took just a few moments for Dean to realize it was somehow the choke chain. He had no idea, nor could he, how much Giv had been devoured by that kind of chain. How he had been beaten furiously by some rootless rage, near strangled while he was lifted from the ground so his front paws hung in grey space between earth and death. How many times did he have to endure attempts to wreck his spirit beyond any capacity to resist? Or be the whipped surrogate of someone's misdirected anger?

Dean could imagine some invisible monster of a human being say . . . *I will bring you to your knees with my power because I am man and of divine issuance. I can buy you, sell you, beat you, exploit you, destroy you. You are nothing more than a drop of rain, and brother, there is an abundance of drops.*

Dean flung the choke chain and leash away. He made sure Giv heard and saw him throwing it far into the dark. They could pick out the faint traces of it landing. But Giv remained as he was, all twisted down and trembling.

A surge of remembered hurt went to the very roots of Sergeant Dean Hickok, late of the U.S. Marines. He had seen this before. Halfway around the world, in young men, after the adrenalin rush of combat is over and they have to breath in all those shattered body parts and savaged lives. Then you go close your eyes to forget, but that burned flesh comes visiting your heart, and you are forcibly taken to a place where there is no body armor to save you.

He had seen it here too, in the streets of America. Once in a vet on crutches. A poor soul sitting at an outdoor food stand. And when a car went by and backfired, this once-upon-a-time soldier crawled up into his clothes and his eyes pinched down and stayed that way until something in his body finally convinced him he was safe.

Dean had been there himself, over many nights, when he woke from sleep helplessly caught up in soaking sheets that felt like the arms of death around him. He would have to sit there in the dark after that, and drink until calmness or dawn came.

The instinct that puts the humane in human had Dean reach out and take hold of Giv even as the dog tried to bend away. It took some time, but Dean eventually got his arms around the dog.

He stroked Giv's muzzle, and he stroked his head. He

eased his hand slowly down the dog's back. He could feel Giv's quivering coat against his bare arms, the heart raging wildly against his own.

But Giv could also feel. He could feel the warmth coming off Dean's hands and arms, and the calmness of a heart next to his own. They remained like that together, till a body of memories calmed and began to unfold, one petalled muscle at a time.

They sat like that, Giv and the Sergeant, as semi's passed in a great arc of headlights and shifting gears and made their way back out onto the roads of America.

They shared one voice, for however temporary. They became this terse unity allied against the reality of their lives, as they walked to the riverfront together—side by side, no chains, solitary yet together.

Dean looked upon the Mississippi for the first time since he was a boy and his family had stopped there while crossing the country. He glanced at Giv who was testing the air. He, too, had once upon a time tasted of the great river.

Dean told Giv how he had stood on these shores with his sister and watched a paddlewheeler pass under the stars, a huge wheel spinning out great reefs of white. The riverboat aglow with lights so it seemed about on fire, while music echoed from the decks and across the night waters. Majestic in that way the untranslatable is majestic, because it speaks to our inborn selves.

Dean sat in the high grass with Giv and went on about how he had tried to get his sister to sneak out of their motel room for a little mischief after their parents went to bed. The parents were in an adjoining room, and Dean's sister wasn't having it and when he threatened to go alone, she got him in a headlock and made him suffer through her book report on Huckleberry Finn and Mark Twain. One of those compulsory "what I did on my summer vacation" numbers. It had been, he told Giv, about as exciting as a postage stamp.

Unable to sleep, Dean drove the river south that night, following the course of the lights along its shore. All those heartrending memories long cloaked in silence came flooding back, and for a little while that night, Sergeant Dean Hickok, late of the U.S. Marines, was a little boy again in the back-seat of his family's beat-up Lincoln. He was watching a nation pass before his eyes in an endless procession of images, and when he breathed in, he could just feel them fill himself up with an infinite capacity to hope and dream. And the light of those years—there is no light like that light. It gathers everyone and everything up in its gold. It is the light which unblemished youth sees best. Yet it can be the first light lost to you.

Dean's eyes began to fill with tears. *I am alone. I am utterly, utterly alone.* Those words—utterly, utterly alone. When you see them written they are one thing; when you hear them they are quite another. But when you are them. He slipped back into their desolate and forsaken reality. He was like a man falling through a great void trying to clutch at memories and reason, just to hang on.

Dean was backsliding way down within himself when something happened which seemed slight and inconsequential. Giv got up from where he was lying in the back. Dean saw him through the rearview mirror. Giv came and put his front paws up on the console and balanced himself between the two front seats.

Nothing like this had happened before. Surprised, Dean said to him, "You look like a hood ornament."

The dog glanced at Dean. How many times have you seen it written, heard a story, saw some documented fact that dogs know when you are in pain, when you hurt, are afraid, or in danger? Giv had felt this one's goodness, just as he had in Mz. El and Anna Perenna and, of course, Ruthie Ruth. He leaned a bit and licked Dean's cheek. That was all. It was his way of saying, I am here, too.

They drove on through the night like that with the warm wind and a beautiful silence.

The powerful loomwork of existence is at work even when you least suspect it. Pain must be shared if it is to be purged from the soul. And to do that, people must live out in the open where others can find them. But in order to be found, one must have faith they can be found, and believe they are worth finding.

⌇

DEAN NEVER HAD a dog, so he had no personal experience in how they humanize you to strangers, or become conduits for easy conversation, and most of all, how they help you bridge that sense of being alone through the tenderness and gratitude they show you. He came to experience what spiritual and physical companions they were.

Dean took the river drive slowly, letting the days mount up. Two-lane blacktops were good; bum roads even better. Wherever coffee shops and motels looked to have washed up on the shores of time was perfect.

Dean would park in the roughs and pack off on foot with Giv, walking for miles well beyond the outskirts of everywhere. Giv grew stronger; his chest filled out and his muscles tautened. Then one day Dean was setting up that makeshift ramp for Giv to get into the SUV and the dog just jumped over it, and that was the end of the ramp.

Next came the stitches, not only his own but Giv's. The hell with a vet or a doctor. Dean was in a Mississippi bar called Little Eva's filing the tips on a pair of needle-nose pliers while he downed a beer and some Jack. Now, filing the tips of pliers in a bar draws some interest and Dean convinced the manager to let him bring Giv in and have some waitress hold a mirror while he extracted his own stitches, so he "wouldn't pluck an eye out before he worked on the dog."

Dean drew a nice little drunken crowd. Everyone said he did a much better job on Giv. Dean was certain that was because he was drunker when he doctored the dog.

Giv was offered a free beer for taking it so well. Dean had learned by then how much Giv liked that first head of foam. Giv wasn't particular either about whether it was imported or domestic beer. To show his appreciation, on the way out, Giv left his mark against the corner of the bar. For this, he received a standing Mississippi ovation.

⁓

THE GATEWAY TO the West . . . the Trail of Tears . . . the hometown of Elvis . . . the fall of the Confederacy at Vicksburg . . . the birthplace of Jazz. The Mississippi was the highway to all of these. Its history stretched over a continent. But the great river, of course, would always be Huckleberry Finn and Mark Twain. They were its literature and legacy. They were the river's foremost creation.

Riding south out of Natchez with shafts of coming light through a picture of summer trees, Dean could feel the world so. It was right here, elegiac and breathing, but . . .

In his mind were questions: Where is *my* place . . . ? What is *my* story . . . ? Will I ever truly be again . . . ? Or do *I* end up a shadow they dust off from time to time as someone says, "See, that was Sergeant Dean Hickok, late of the U.S. Marines."

Sometimes answers arrive as unexpected memories. There was a time when Dean had faced the unenviable task alone of cleaning out his sister's closets after her death. She had been one of those who saved everything: letters, snapshots, report cards, yearbooks, her cheerleader outfit, mementos of every kind, and doodads whose value would be a mystery to the most formidable mind. Among those boxes, he'd discovered the book report she had written that summer.

As he'd sat there reading, the sister he knew, the one who had headlocked and harassed him, was alive again in all the pure bounty of her eleven years. She had included in her book report a quote from Twain about the river that had made him so famous, "The face of the water, in time, became a wonderful book . . . and it was not a book to be read once and thrown aside, for it had a new story to tell every day."

In those few sentences were vast promises and imperishable dreams. The part missing inside him was the dream. And the dream is always indispensable. It is an essential character to every drama for it restores the physical world to its rightful place in life.

17

THE BLESSING OF THE ANIMALS

H E SEES THE *dog climb over the console and, just like that, take up residence in the shotgun seat. This is the first time Giv had come up front.*

He perfectly triangulated himself with the sun, and the breeze. He took to watching, absorbing the landscape and its smells with a pronounced interest. He did eventually glance at Dean, as if at least to acknowledge his presence. Dean thought he saw a limitless satisfaction in the dog's stare.

Dean had Ruthie's last known address, and he'd mapped out how to get there. He saw New Orleans for the first time from the highway, until he got off at Pontchartrain and started north into the parish by the 17th Street Canal.

Dean had no idea what he would come upon. He'd seen Katrina and its effects on television while he was stationed in Iraq, but two years later, to drive these streets and witness the silent geography of such destruction. It was a world unfit, a world of endless waste, a world beaten into oblivion then boarded up. Block after block of sorrow heaped on with the weight of hearts and revolting pyres of forgotten garbage. Abandoned home after abandoned home, a dirge not only of monstrous misfortune, but of unforgiving indifference.

This couldn't be America, not our America, not the America so many fought for. Not the America that birthed one of the most precious events in world history. Not the America that professed to be at one with the speeches of God. Not the America that surmounted every mountain and carried its helpless with it all the way. This, he thought, was more like Baghdad.

When they neared Mz. El's house, Giv grew unsettled and the sounds he made as they pulled up to the address, Dean would not easily forget. Words came to mind like anticipation and torment. When Dean got out of the SUV, he noted the orange scrawl on the front door which meant someone had died there.

Dean had left a window open enough and Giv, he squeezed and twisted his way clear and jumped then dashed up the yard to where he stood on his hind legs and clawed at the front door. Dean grabbed Giv, but he fought and escaped and sped around to the back leaping a rotted couch.

He started after the dog, jumping from the wooden porch where it had caved away. He could see the grim stain of a waterline along the second floor. Scents of decay and rot seeped through the window boards. He was partway around the place when someone yelled, "You there . . . Hey, you there."

Dean turned to see a policeman getting out of a squad car.

"Can I help you?" asked the policeman.

Dean pointed to the house. The officer was staring at him suspiciously. Dean suddenly felt very uncomfortable, "I was . . . looking for someone."

"Here?"

"Yes."

The officer rested a hand on his holster belt. Dean could hear the officious crackle of leather, "Who?"

"A girl. A young woman actually."

"She have a name?"

"Officer, I wasn't—"

"Does-she-have-a—"

Before he finished, he saw past Dean. Giv was maneuvering a pile of detritus against the house wall. "Giv," yelled the policeman. "Giv . . . is that you?"

When the dog saw him, he raced over and the policeman kneeled and put out his arms, "This is Giv, right?"

"Yes," said Dean.

The man was near to tears, he was that happy.

"I was trying to find Ruthie Ruth," said Dean, "and get her dog back to her. Do you know her?"

RAFER NOW LIVED in a FEMA trailer parked in his front yard. He invited Dean over so they could trade stories.

They sat at the dinette drinking beer, the partly roofless and mud-ruined walls of his home commanding the view from his trailer window. "Yeah," said Rafer, "that's the first thing I see every morning. Twenty years of mortgage."

"Will the area ever really come back?"

"My mother thought so." Rafer pointed to a photo in a pewter frame. Mz. El stood outside a church in a white linen dress. Her hands were folded together. "My mother was never deterred by reality. Ruthie's death, that hit her hard. As hard as my youngest brother's death."

They talked through sunset and dinner, and Rafer detailed Ruthie's life from a childhood at Disney World to her death in Katrina. Rafer spoke of her as if she were some cherished baby sister. Dean learned about Dallas, and about Ian and his brother Jem, and how Giv had been stolen.

Dean asked, "There's still nothing about what happened to her boyfriend?"

"My opinion," said Rafer. "The brother probably killed him."

"Where is Jem now?"

"Oklahoma State Penitentiary," Rafer explained. "Jem had been living with some fringers around the University and he'd been supplementing his income, as he had for years, by committing burglaries. One night Jem ends up robbing some steroid-freak wrestler who came home five minutes too soon. Jem is doing twenty to life for murder."

They walked to Mz. El's house after dark. At night the neighborhood was a ghost town of mummified dwellings and an uneasy place to walk through for Dean, as it spoke to his time in war. Giv knew where they were going and led the way.

"He still likes that first head of foam on a beer," said Rafer. "Isn't that something?"

Dean told Rafer about the night at Little Eva's, and Rafer's laugh carried down through the remains of naked and silent front yards.

Rafer aimed his searchlight on the back of the house. Vines had grown over the face of things. The tree still protruded from the second story. Its branches had died; the trunk had whitened. But the visual—it was more akin to the annals of war.

In the dark, Rafer asked, "What are you gonna do with Giv now?"

"My intention was to get him home," said Dean.

"Home," said Rafer. "Where is that?"

⁓

"WHAT HAPPENED after Katrina?" asked Dean. "Do you have any idea how Giv got to Kentucky?"

A slightly drunk and deeply moved Rafer had Dean follow him. In the corner of his bedroom, covered carefully by plastic tarps, were five stacked boxes. "These," said Rafer, "these . . . are filled with lives. All Ruthie's work. Her drawings. Stories. E-mail letters from her to my mother, from my mother to her. The brothers' music. Their CD. Ian's music. Pictures. My mother made sure . . ."

He took the boxes and began to drop each on the bed where he could get at them. "I forgot which one has . . ."

Giv climbed up on the bed and began sniffing away. And Dean . . . The boxes held him captive; they made him think of his sister. That was exactly like her, saving all those personal secret treasures.

"My mother kept all this for a reason," said Rafer. "I haven't answered your question about Giv. But I'm looking for something that will, in part, anyway."

The box he was rummaging through at that moment had loose snapshots. One he handed to Dean, "While I'm looking, check this out."

It was of a girl and a boy posing with Giv in front of a shop that did body art.

"Ruthie?"

"And Ian. The picture was taken in Dallas at the beginning of that summer. Ruthie worked there as an artist. It's the only picture we have of them together."

It was a simple and unassuming picture really, except for one thing. It was the kind of photo that almost everyone has tucked away somewhere in their own heart. The one that stirs up the years and has you lying there at night longing for what the depths of real passion were like. Dean had been about their age when he enlisted, a little older perhaps, but not by much. He suddenly flashed on those fresh-faced grunts in training camp, of whom he had been one.

"I found it," said Rafer. He held up a CD, "A German documentary crew filmed this."

As Rafer opened his laptop on the dinette table he explained what Dean was about to see.

"My mother contacted Ruthie's parents. They came. My mother asked if they wanted Giv, they did not. Giv was brokenhearted. He loved Ruthie like nothing else. He hardly ate or drank, and just lay at the door like he was waiting. Dogs die of broken hearts. You read about it all the time. My mother had a plan to deal with it. You'll see on the documentary.

"We were all camped out at a friend of my mother's whose place was habitable. And one day my mother says, 'I'd appreciate you going into the garage; there's an old red wagon in there. I want you to bring it and put the dog in it.' I say, 'Mama, what are you doing?' And my mother says, 'I'm gonna get that dog well.' I ask her, 'How you gonna do that?' and she says, 'You'll see when we get back,' and she's gonna pull the dog in that wagon. I ask her, 'I'll drive you all if you need to get somewhere,' and she answers me in that way she had, 'I pray better when I'm walking.'"

The CD was ready. Rafer filled Dean in on a few last details. His mother had started off after Rafer left for work. She was going to a church nearly seven blocks away. It was a hot day and a slow, miserable walk, especially for a seventy-five-year-old woman pulling that wagon.

Mz. El had gone about a block before a crew of young boys with unbound energy saw this curiosity and asked Mz. El, "What gives?"

Now, Mz. El, she could zone right in on children and tap their essence. She had always given out the absolute airtight lowdown, like it or not. Giv had lost his home, she said. He had lost his best friend. He was down and in need. Those boys, they had all been to that place, young as they were, and they voted, street style, to help push that wagon to the church.

A block later, two girls on bicycles who knew the boys rode by and wondered, "What gives?"

Well, the next thing those girls are walking their bikes alongside the wagon and leaning down and kissing Giv soft and lovely, as only little girls can do, promising him it will be all right.

By the next block a young mother with a stroller passed by and recognized Mz. El and called to her. She had been one of the old woman's students. One of the many Mz. El had bewildered and demanded and outright loved an education into. She was one of the many who had been preached to, *Be the Miracle*. Well, now one of Mz. El's girls was pushing that stroller, and this young mother, she had hold of the wagon with Mz. El as they pulled it to the church.

Rafer pressed play. Music over black. A single, simple piano refraining an old spiritual—"Let Us Break Bread Together." Words fade in on the screen:

Children of the Nation
New Orleans

The black screen gives way to a street. Houses hit hard by Katrina but still habitable; trees hold the sun at bay.

From porches and windows, touches of humanity. Then the camera frames up this odd caravan of children around an old woman and a red wagon bearing a dog.

At that point, the camera came close and framed Mz. El and the interviewer asked, "What is all this . . ."

Mz. El, worn from the long walk said, "Like so many of us who suffered the hurricane, this dog has lost his home and someone he loved. And we're gonna try and make him well."

"Where are you going?"

She pointed toward a wooden steeple.

The camera zoomed in on a listless Giv as the wagon trundled over barely serviceable sidewalk. It cut to Mz. El as she was asked her name.

"My name," she said, "is unimportant. I am just another child of the nation trying to make the way."

The interviewer went from child to child after that, and they told their stories of devastation and the unreal fears the hurricane had made all too real. But as they spoke, you got more than a fleeting glimpse revealed in their faces and manner, of the limitless treasure people have within to endure and then go on.

The camera became part of the processional. The church they walked to had been lovely, once upon a time, but now it was a closed edifice of clapboard with clerestory windows abused as target practice.

There was, though, in the shady lot beside the church a huge menagerie of people, dogs, cats and hung between the church's outer triforium and the branches of a grand tree was a sign: *The Blessings of the Animals.*

The music on the soundtrack was actually coming from a loudspeaker on the church steps. The camera worked the crowd as only cameras can. People held up snapshots of their pet friends. *This is my . . . I lost my . . . Have you seen my . . .*

Was it any different emotionally, Dean thought, than people like himself walking through the ashes of 9/11 with snapshots of loved ones trembling in the lightning flash of police and ambulance lights, imploring strangers . . . *This is my . . . I lost my . . . Have you seen my . . .*

Mz. El pulled that wagon through a congregation of the ravaged which knew no bounds—neither by race, nor sex, nor beliefs. And while she stood in line for Giv to be blessed, those waiting with her poured out goodwill and affection. Person to person, pet to pet, living soul to living soul.

A woman approached with a cat, and Rafer told Dean, "That's the S.O.B. I told you about . . . Bullet." The woman put the cat in the wagon and Bullet began to lick Giv's face.

You are never alone; even if you are the blackest spot at the deepest center of the sun, you are never alone. Every living heart is a kinsman in waiting, every solitary face a friend moving toward you through that desolate space known as despair, and for every anguished heart there is an answer, complete with living sky and heaven.

Giv's neck rose stiffly as Bullet licked his muzzle and his eyes and his ears while Mz. El whispered to him and the children stroked him and he could smell on the warm wind his kind everywhere. And Dean witnessed the faintest change in Giv's eyes as one might the slightest movement at the very edges of the horizon, and Giv's tail . . . it lifted, only a trace really, but it lifted.

This was a moment, Dean thought, he'd never had as a soldier who'd suffered. He had never been part of some congregation of souls who came together to deal with their flag-draped coffins. What he was witnessing as part of a German documentary—that was America, that was our nation. The nation was never some human footrace toward a grey nonsense; its power was communion.

⌐

RAFER STOPPED THE documentary right there. "That November," he said, "my mother had a stroke. A serious one. She couldn't walk or feed herself. She'd lost the ability to speak. To see her, of all people, like that. She was in assisted care out in La Place. It was the hardest thing I've had to do.

"I was pretty overwhelmed then. My mother, no place to live, this city. The woman with the cat." He looked at Giv with a trace of guilt. "She offered to take Giv. She was moving to Arkansas. At least I think it was Arkansas. She had a son-in-law with some land. The last I saw or knew of Giv was that Thanksgiving."

Rafer stood and went to the refrigerator. He brought out the last two beers. Dean noticed how Rafer's glance drifted toward those boxes on the bed.

"What's the saying, you know, growing old ain't for sissies." Rafer shook his head. "They had that right."

He handed Dean a beer, but he did not sit himself. Rather he walked partway down the length of the trailer. His focus now was purely on those boxes. "My mother made me promise that I would try to do something with Ruthie's art work, her stories. Ian's music. She wanted them to . . . maybe have their day in this world. Some form of recognition." He leaned against the bathroom door, partly drunk. "I knew it was unrealistic but I promised. I'm a fifty-four-year-old policeman living in a FEMA trailer. I don't even know how to begin to do something like she wanted. I lie there at night looking at those boxes and I see my mother." He turned to Dean, his stare fixed, "But you . . ."

"What?"

"You're twenty-four. You want to be a journalist, right?"

"You're not thinking . . ."

"You're a veteran. A war hero. You want to be a journalist. You'll meet the right kind of people."

"No—"

"And the right kind of people will want to meet you."

"I came here to bring Giv home."

"Yeah," said Rafer. He looked at Giv stretched out there on the floor. "It would be a lot to ask of someone."

Rafer came and sat across the table from Dean. He folded his hands and air expelled from his nose. "But . . . a man who would travel out of his way one thousand miles to bring a dog that wasn't his, to a woman he never met, at an address he couldn't even be sure was still hers. Of course, what I'm asking would be a huge responsibility."

"Yes."

"Do you believe in fate?"

"No."

"What might have gone down if Giv hadn't been on the road that night?"

"Color me . . . a casualty."

"As a policeman, my personal experience, life is painted with fate. My mother, she would say, 'Fate is what happens while you're busy making choices.' Well," said Rafer, "at least you have *your* dream."

That word . . .

"A dream *is* mandatory," said Dean. "But so is more beer." Dean stood. "I'll get it."

As he went for the door, Giv also stood and fell in line with him, but Dean laced his fingers around the top of Giv's neck and held him back. "All right," he asked Rafer, "I leave him here with you?"

"Why not? We're family."

Dean made his way to the SUV, and Giv barked after him.

Rafer called to Dean from inside the screen door, "Sergeant . . ."

Dean stopped and looked around. "If you don't come back," said Rafer, "I'll understand. It'll be all right."

⁓

HAD RAFER PICKED up on something in Dean's reaction at wanting to be alone? It struck Dean—had he without even realizing, meant to leave?

He drove around the corner and pulled over at the edge of Fleurs de Lis Park. A few, lone, houselights here and there stood out. The rest of the homes were just darkened crypts. He studied it all with great circumspection.

So many dreams lost in battle that could not be resurrected. He felt such complete failure with what had been his original duty. He thought of Giv also. Giv had not been able to save Ruthie Ruth from the flood, as Dean had not been able to save his own soldiers on the banks of the Euphrates.

Dean sat there in the windless dark, with his hands folded on the steering wheel, struggling to gather up all those disparate voices that exist in secret battles within and somehow find order, meaning, value.

A dream often needs someone who has lived and suffered and so could understand and sympathize, who could look into a few boxes of forgotten hopes and find the world.

Sergeant Dean Hickok, late of the U.S. Marines, did not fully comprehend yet, that the dream he was searching for had found him.

After stocking up on beer, Dean drove back to the house. As Dean came around a corner by the park, a dog went sprinting up the sidewalk in the opposite direction.

The asphalt smoked with tire rubber as Dean stopped short. He leapt from the SUV and yelled, "Giv!"

The dog did such a fast pivot he lost his balance and slid along the sidewalk like something drunk on ice skates. He then began running back toward Dean.

"Where the hell were you going?"

The dog didn't stop when he got to Dean; instead, he ran past him and with one leap had himself in the open SUV window. He pulled the last bit of himself in and when Dean slipped behind the wheel Giv was propped up in the shot-gun seat and panting wildly.

⁓

"FROM THE MOMENT you were gone," Rafer told Dean upon his return, "he stood at the door pushing at the screen and going from window to window, no matter what I said, and finally he just used that skull of his and punched that flimsy excuse of a door nearly off its hinges."

They drank more beer and Rafer brought forth from a drawer these thin and expensive cigarillos that an officer friend had "confiscated" in a bust.

"I didn't mean to pressure you, son. About the boxes. It's just . . . I feel I failed my mother in a way."

Dean went to bed that night on a poor excuse of a couch by the dinette, where the boxes were stacked up under a trace of moonlight. Giv was there also asleep on the floor under that very same trace of moonlight. And Dean's sister, she was there also. It was as if that family trip along the great river and the book report she'd written all those years ago had happened with one purpose.

Sometimes with darkness come all forms of possibility that shadow whisper across your soul. Often they are just hints slipping through you between silence and sleep.

How could he give voice to them? Ruthie . . . Ian . . . even Jem. How could he resurrect them out of those boxes? He also understood this would be about resurrecting himself.

Somewhere in between the sleep and the silence, his mind worked itself back to that razor-headed dog leading those sheep through a firefight along the Euphrates, amidst dust and burning carnage. The moment was still raw and powerful in his imagination, and he could feel it all the way down into the guts of the earth and completely inseparable from his own existence.

Then he looked at Giv there under a trace of moonlight, and the will of an idea surfaced that made him sit up.

Giv was the journey. He would be, as Twain wrote, "The face of the water."

When Dean and Giv left New Orleans the next day, those five boxes had been loaded into the back of the SUV. And as he headed west to Barrett Junction, California, he already knew, in his heart, he would write this story.

18

OKLAHOMA STATE PENITENTIARY

SEE THE SNAPSHOT of Giv between Ruthie and Ian outside the Body Politique. Dean had clipped it to the dash; it would be his gateway to the future. As he made his way west, he had also embarked upon those boxes in the quiet of motel rooms. He went through their contents with a soldierly determination. Each drawing and song, each story idea, child's book, all e-mails and letters. He meant to experience them all until they felt like part of his own personal history.

On his way to California, Dean decided to stop in Dallas and research the haunts of Ruthie and Ian's short time there together. It also occurred to him to try and meet with Jem.

Oklahoma State Penitentiary is a maximum security prison. Access to inmates is extraordinarily difficult, and for a non-family member, a near impossibility.

While driving to Dallas, Dean evolved a plan. He would write Jem, detailing who he was, how he'd come upon Giv, and the reason why he wanted to meet. He also decided not to mention anything about Ian's disappearance and Jem's potential guilt.

At the same, time he tracked down the boys' parents to solicit their help. Jem's father had written him off, and he hung up on Dean almost immediately. The mother, on the other hand, had remained close to her son. Not just out of a mother's sense of loyalty, but because she hoped one day Jem would open his heart enough for her to find out what had happened to Ian, and there could be some form of closure.

She was the one who contacted the Warden to try and arrange a meeting, being realistic enough to know the odds were small that this soldier would learn anything.

Dean was in Dallas when he got word. He had gone to Dealey, the 6th Floor of the Book Depository, Deep Elum, he'd met Stoner. The Body Politique was still there, though "Trees" was gone.

As for the Body Politique, Dean and Giv had become accustomed to walking side by side without a leash, but when they were on the block where the Body Politique was, Giv just took off and Dean could not get him to stop; he was left only to lay chase. Giv led him right to the storefront, his body intense and excited to get inside as if someone he cared for would be found in there waiting.

At the door Dean had to take hold of Giv, who strained relentlessly to get in that shop. They do not forget, they are not beasts that just endure and die. They *are* part of the same river of sorrows and farewells that affect us all.

⁓

WARDEN JAMES D. Love was a twenty-year veteran of the Oklahoma Correctional System. Dean was ushered into Warden Love's office. He was a thin and straightforward man, the perfect, small-town professional father.

On the walls were the usual photos of him with local politicians and members of law enforcement. But two of them did stand out. One was of Farrah Fawcett from the *Charlie's Angels* years with Warden Love at a charity benefit in Las Vegas. The other was a signed photo of Isaac Hayes in all his *Shaft* glory.

Then Warden Love showed Dean a photo that he kept on his desk. "My daughter Kitty is serving in Iraq."

There she was, somewhere in Fallujah, with her K-9 dog.

"He's a Belgian Malinois. Kitty trained in Pendleton. I'm so proud of her. I'm so proud of everyone who has served."

The Warden then went over to a bureau and pulled out a portfolio that was filled with newspaper clips. He called Dean over.

"*Stars and Stripes,*" said Warden Love. "I cut out articles where soldiers have showed exemplary honor." He took one and handed it to Dean. "When Jem's mother told me you were a Marine hero who was wounded in Iraq, I did some research."

There was the article written about U.S. Marine Sergeant Dean Hickok's heroic defense of a bridge on the Euphrates. The photo they had used was one of him taken just days before at Camp Longbow. The Dean Hickok there seemed almost a stranger, and the article . . . At moments like this he was powerless against the reality of such loss. He handed the article back to Warden Love.

"I'm honored to meet you, son."

The Warden could hear Dean choke up a bit when he said, "Thank you, sir. But I am the least of them, I assure you."

The Warden put a hand on the young man's back and had him sit.

"Your service . . . and saving that dog's life on the road, are the reasons I'm allowing this meeting."

DEAN WOULD ONLY be allowed to talk with Jem through a glass partition. An officer escorted him to where he was to sit and wait. The basics of protocol were explained and then the officer left. The room itself was painted a befitting dour grey. Dean did not have to wait long before Jem appeared on the other side of the glass partition.

Considering the history and circumstances of his life, Jem looked to Dean noticeably young, even for his age, which was only twenty-one. He was also quite handsome, better looking, in fact, than the snapshots his mother had e-mailed Dean.

"So," said Jem. "You ended up with Giv."

"Maybe the better way of saying it would be Giv ended up with me."

"In your letter you said you found him on a road in Kentucky."

"In a rainstorm. He had been locked in a crate in a shed. He escaped it. He was in rough shape."

"Kentucky. Of all places. That dog must have nine lives. The girl, what was her name again?"

"Ruthie . . . Ruthie Ruth."

"She was a runaway."

"Yeah."

"She died, right?"

"In Katrina. During an animal rescue. She drowned."

"What a fool. For a stinkin' animal." Jem eyed Dean. "I guess that's not exactly the politically correct thing to say."

Dean kept his emotions to himself, as this was an "interview" with a purpose.

"In your letter, you said you were a Marine."

"That's right. A sergeant."

"You served in Iraq?"

"Yes."

"You know a guardsman named Stoner? Charlie Stoner. He was from Dallas."

"I never met him. I was told about Charlie by his brother."

"Right, you were in Dallas?"

"Like I wrote you. I wanted to meet everyone who was part of Giv's life. I wanted to see the places—like Deep Elum."

"What's the point?"

"You, Giv, me, Ruthie . . ."

He watched as Jem sat back and just stared at him, somewhat blankly, somewhat mysteriously. "The dog was more my brother's than mine."

Dean was certain of one thing—Jem expected him now to start talking about Ian. But he did not. "You still into music?"

Jem touched his heart. "Unfortunately, I'm on my own planet here. This place is about hillbilly or n———r rap. They don't know Curt Cobain from the friggin' Pope. They got a rodeo here. A rodeo. This is crackerville. A rodeo. It's a yearly thing. You should check it out. The inmates have teams, champions. The arena is right beyond this cellblock. It's a big deal. The 'necks come from all over the county with their donut-assed wives and little inbreds. Sit in the stands. You can feel your IQ dropping."

"I heard some of your tapes."

"Mine?"

"Ruthie left behind possessions. Among them was a CD you and Ian did. And recording sessions. The ones done in Dallas, I gather."

"We did our best work there. Ian wrote a couple of songs. I wrote a couple."

"Yea. There were sets. The two of you together. Tapes of Ian alone and tapes of you alone."

"What? You have solo tapes of mine?"

"Yes."

Jem was visibly interested and decidedly intense. "Mine . . . just me."

"Yes."

"They were the only copies. I didn't know what happened to them. I didn't know they were missing until after Ian . . . disappeared."

Jem was all wired up about that tape. So, Dean decided not to approach the question of Ian's disappearance yet, but just to leave it there.

"Could you make copies and get them to me?"

"I don't see why not. Unless the prison—"

"I'm working on a new CD. Hardcore white stuff. And those Dallas sessions would fit perfectly."

"I wanted to ask you something about Giv."

"Giv . . . he sure didn't like me much."

"You stole him, right?"

"Yeah."

"Where'd you steal him from?"

Jem's mouth kind of pinched in a little. "It was a motel."

"Do you remember the name?"

"No, it was in New Mexico, or maybe Arizona. One of those nowhere places that need a good fumigating."

"Who did the dog belong to?"

"The bitch who ran the joint."

"Why *that* dog?"

"Ian liked him."

"Ian," said Dean. And he said the name in a way that emphasized it.

"I can't believe you have those tapes. Talk about good fortune."

"The real good fortune, when you think about it, is that if it wasn't for Giv, I wouldn't be here," said Dean. "And so, no tapes."

Dean saw that what he just said had landed like a blow. What was Jem thinking? Dean wanted to ask but he waited a bit. What Jem might well be thinking, of course, was that if it wasn't for Giv, he might not be there himself.

"Something bother you about what I said?"

As if the question did not exist, Jem asked, "My mother said you were wounded in Iraq."

"I lost a kidney."

"She said you won medals."

"Yes."

"It must be something to have people see you as a hero."

"It has its drawbacks."

"Name me one."

"Medals are achieved during combat, which means all around you, friends are being wounded, crippled *and* killed."

"You ever kill someone?"

"Yes," said Dean. "A number of men."

"What did it feel like? Inside, I mean. For you."

Dean leaned forward. "How did it feel for you?"

Jem leaned back and looked away. He seemed utterly cut off. "You gonna write this as a book?"

"A book maybe, an article . . . I'm not sure."

"We all gonna be in it? Me, my brother?"

"Everyone who has had the dog. That's why I was even asking you about where you stole it from."

"Why this dog?"

"You might say he saved my life."

"He saved your life. How did he do that? You said you found him on a road in Kentucky."

"I was thinking about committing suicide that night."

Jem blinked.

"See, I've killed men. I've seen those closest to me wasted, crippled, dead. My sister went down in Tower Two on 9/11. To have suffered or caused death can have a profound impact on one's life. But you know that as well as I."

For Jem this was suddenly like looking into his own conscience. "Okay, so the dog saved your life. Why the story at all?"

"It . . . feels of America somehow."

Jem considered.

"We're all part of America, at this time," said Dean. "Aren't we?"

"This interview, what we're talking about now will be part of it?"

"Yes."

"My music. Me. My dreams. You'd put that there, too?"

"Yes."

"How do I know you're gonna keep your word?"

"What would the story be without you, Jem?"

Jem suddenly looked down at his hands. Dean noticed they were picking out chords on an invisible guitar. The hungers that shape a human mind.

"I assume any conversation about me is gonna have to include—"

"You can talk to me, you could write to me. But I expect anything you want to get out about Ian *will* end outside the Arcadia Coffee Shop behind the Courthouse where you . . . *last saw him.*"

Dean said nothing more. There was only the silence of what might, if anything, come next. Dean had approached it almost militarily. Take up your position and wait. He wished he could evaluate Jem's body language, or any minute physical tic, but he could not.

"I didn't do it," Jem said quite matter-of-factly. "But . . . if I had done it. This is how it could have happened."

Jem began but he spoke in the third person, as if he and Ian were players in a drama or a film unfolding before his eyes.

The ride out of Dallas, he said, had been damn quiet and lonely. Even bleak. The heat didn't help and the van AC had busted. The ride kept getting more miserable and tense.

Ian took it upon himself to apologize again and again until Jem just choked off that talk. The drive was marked by sadness and farewell. They were closed rooms now—two strangers that shared a last name. Ian had basically allowed Jem to take him to New Orleans, rather than admit he had this session job lined up. He did not want to hurt his brother, but he also did not want to incur his wrath.

At Tyler they stopped for lunch. They ended up at the Arcadia Coffee Shop, which was just behind the court-house and, not coincidentally, a block or so from the Greyhound Bus Terminal.

After they ordered, Jem told Ian that he had to go back to the van for his cell phone. While Ian sat in the coffee shop, Jem unloaded Ian's belongings and put them on the sidewalk. When Jem returned, the food had arrived and they ate. Jem put out a lot of goodwill toward his brother during that lunch, but as they finished, Jem said, "From here, wouldn't it make just as much sense to go directly to Memphis?"

There should be a snapshot of Ian at that moment. He looked like he did when the old man would come down on him . . . "Wallpaper". . . that's what the old man would call him.

Then Jem had said, "You got the wallpaper look, homey."

Ian tried to give out with some pissant excuse about "not wanting to see Jem hurt."

"You must think I was plainly stupid," Jem told him, "and you could run that story. I knew when you slinked off with Stoner something was going down and I was out. People got too much with the cha-cha lips, you know . . . wallpaper."

Ian followed Jem out of the Arcadia, keeping a safe dis-tance and remaining quiet. Jem looked back at him with contempt. They had parked up from the Arcadia just into a side street.

Rounding the corner Ian saw his suitcases on the sidewalk. He ran to the van. "What are you doing?"

"I'm getting you out of my life."

"Is what happened my fault? Tell me, Jem. How is it—?"

Jem hit the automatic unlock.

"I need my guitars," said Ian.

"You need—"

Jem was in the van and getting ready to lock Ian out, but Ian was too quick. The two brothers faced off there in the front seats.

"I need my two guitars. My share of the other equipment, you don't want me to have it, okay. But I need my guitars."

Jem said nothing. He just stared at his brother. He could see Ian was frightened now that there would be a confrontation. Jem did not know what angered him more, his brother's cowardice or his selfishness.

Ian climbed over the engine to get to his equipment. As he did, Jem kicked at him. Ian saw the kick and reacted. He threw out his arm in a blocking motion but the hand caught Jem across the face. And that was it.

The fight went down right there in the back of the van. If you want to call it that. Ian did all he could to defend himself, but Jem hit him again and again till Ian lay there stunned. But it wasn't enough.

Jem kneeled on Ian's chest and took volley shots at his brother's face. Long, slow and direct blows until Ian finally blacked out. But that wasn't enough.

Something had exploded inside Jem. He wanted to hurt Ian more. In a box were spools of heavy-duty electrical and gaffer's tape. Jem bound his brother's hands behind his back. He did the same to his nose and mouth, winding the tape around his brother's head until Ian was only a mask of eyes. Then he drove away with Ian in the back, leaving the suitcases on the sidewalk.

After the disappearance, a shop owner would be able to say she saw someone unloading suitcases from the van, which would back up Jem's claim that he'd left Ian on a Tyler street corner near the bus station. That was a pure stroke of luck that would play in Jem's favor.

You would think Jem should be in a state of panic, unable to think, but that was not the case. He was sure and focused. To see his brother's fear when he came to and found himself bound and gagged in the back of the moving van. There was a pleasure in that, a just pleasure.

At some point Jem thought he would undo Ian, but the more he struggled and suffered the more Jem wanted to have him suffer and struggle. Then the suffering and struggling just stopped as the breathing stopped. Ian's legs and torso jerked, and there was this odd sound coming through the tape. Then there was nothing at all. Ian lay there like the "wallpaper" he was.

Around Tyler there are plenty of dead towns and long roads bleeding off to forgotten quarries and abandoned homesteads. If there is one thing Texas has, it's oceans of earth.

Jem dug a grave using his brother's guitar. He placed the body in the shallow pit after taking all his identification. He siphoned gas from the tank and set his brother on fire. This was done near dusk. As the flames subsided, he used Ian's guitar to shovel back the dirt.

19

A Soldier's Godfathers

S EE THE MESAS *of the west, riven as they are with red clay rising out of an endless expanse and imagine Giv against that eternal backdrop.*

They are driving through the country of Giv's youth, and Dean wonders, is there inside Giv some grand memory of time and place? Does the perfume of dry sage and desert air take him back to the heart of his birth? Does there exist in Giv some fixed longing, like that in man, for the first true home?

The west they are traveling is a land suffering with drought. There have been fires in Texas and Kansas. There will be in Utah and in California. At Tahoe, Inyo, Big Pine, Independence. It is land hungry for water.

Dean had promised John Hernandez he would be in Barrett Junction for the 4th of July. John Hernandez was the father of one of Dean's squad mates, Corporal Randy Hernandez, who had been killed in the assault along the Euphrates. Dean would be meeting the gentleman for the first time, not only to pay his respects, but because Mr. Hernandez was in need of hearing all he could about his son.

Barrett Junction is about half an hour east of San Diego and just outside the Cleveland National Forest. It is also, as they say, "down the hill" about fifteen miles from Tecate and the border. This is classic California backcountry, written about in Sunset and Westways and hard-core traveling mags like Friction Time. It's a place of chaparral and acacia and great stands of pepper trees that bristle in the heat. There are pines rising singular and solemn on hills that look to have been sculpted by artisans from the age of iron. The sky is a pure and cloudless blue, and in the deeps of gullies the clearwater streams of winter become the dry rock trails of summer.

There was a calmness to the place Dean felt right away. The kind of deep and abiding calmness that would hold against the upheavals of time.

⁓

THE TOWN WAS a handful of roadside buildings and the **Barrett Junction Cafe, Home Of The Famous Fish Fry and All You Can Eat Country Breakfast Buffet.**

He had been told to watch for a trailer court ringed by pepper trees on Highway 94. Just past it, Dean would see Hermosita Road.

Little beautiful—that's what Hermosita meant, and Dean

was to follow that winding cut up into the hills. There were a few homes scattered among the scrub and pine. Mostly small and rough affairs with corrals or trailers dumped down on cement pads, with monster satellite dishes that looked like they were meant to pick up Radio Free Mars.

Hernandez had a double-wide about three quarters of a mile from Barrett Lake. A cabin of some kind was set back behind it in a grove of trees. The front yard Dean pulled into was hardened sand that crunched under his wheels then kicked up, so the air was heavy with it when he and Giv got out of the car.

John Hernandez filled his doorway, and made it look like something outfitted for children. He was a tall, huge man with a deep thick chest, who wore Hawaiian shirts that would fit as well on a dinosaur. He had an enormous shaved head and grey red goatee, "Sergeant. It's so damn good . . ."

Big John, which is what his friends called him, didn't bother finishing. He clasped Dean's hand and pulled the kid to him and embraced him in a mauling hug that was absolute masculine affection.

Now, Hernandez had been a master sergeant and five-alarm lifer, and Dean was emotionally overcome and called Big John, "Sir."

"Sir, hell. By the way, my little one has been two feet off the ground waiting for you to get here." He looked down at Giv. "And who's this rugged-looking character?"

Hernandez bent down and patted Giv on the chest so hard you could hear the echo clear down to the trailer park.

"Let me show you your digs, then we'll unpack and get down to sporting a few drinks."

He led Dean along a gravel pathway around the double-wide to that grove of trees where stood the small log cabin with a porch.

Where the light through the door captured their shadows and fell upon the far wall was a photo, blown-up to poster size, of Randy in a football uniform being flanked by his father and younger brother, who was named Slip.

Dean pointed to the photo, and the big man took a breath but his chest seemed to resist the effort. "That was at the league championship game. Randy left six weeks later for boot camp. We built this place together. It was prefab. We figured after Randy came home, he'd have his own place, you know, but we'd *all* still be together."

Big John put his arm around Dean, and they stood silently before the photo, this mortal chain of men who had experienced the dark luster of war.

It was then that Slip, the younger brother, arrived. He was closing in on nine. Thin and somewhat small for his age, he was called Slip because as a child, he constantly gave his folks "the slip." He had a penchant for freewheeling. Take your eyes off him, he was into a cupboard, under a bureau, out the door, scaling a bumper to get into the back of the pickup or trailing up into the hills like some diapered Daniel Boone.

Randy had often told Dean about his kid brother. "My folks stitched bells on his shoes and on the back of his shirts so they could always hear him. But Slip was wicked smart and stripped 'em off. After that, the old man strung a cable across the front yard and hooked up the poor bugger. Man, was Slip miserable. Then someone 'accidentally' left one of those long, tree-branch clippers where Slip could find it. It was a pisser to watch him figure out how to chop through the cable."

Dean knew that the boy had been born with cerebral palsey, and as Slip entered the cabin all juiced with excitement, Dean watched how one leg bent in at the knee so the boy was forced to get along balancing on the front part of his foot. The boy's left arm, it crooked at the elbow and so perpetually dangled across his chest.

Even though Slip was all wrapped up in excitement at having Dean there, he was the absolute composed adult when he put out a hand to shake, and said, "I'm very proud to meet you, sir." Of course, when it came to Giv, he showed no such restraint. Slip dove over the back of the couch and Giv leapt up to meet him.

That evening, Hernandez barbecued on the back patio. Steaks with sides of macaroni and cheese and tater tots. Thanks to Slip, Dean discovered Giv could snare a tater tot out of the air like nobody's business. All parties decided he had either been part of some secret tater-tot-snagging-experiment or was the ultimate natural.

Dinner conversation was devoted mostly to Randy. Stories meant to give off good feeling, kick off laughter or make you say "no way." The last hours of that last surge on the Euphrates were clearly left for another time.

Slip asked if he could take Giv and tramp up into the hills and show him the obelisk at Shepherd's Point. Dean was fine with that, and Slip asked did Giv need a leash. That prompted Dean to tell him about the choke chain and how it had affected the dog, and all agreed to forgo such trappings.

Then Slip, as he was setting off with the dog, told Dean, "When I was a boy my father made me wear a leash, and I feel the same way as Giv."

"Make it sound like something it isn't in front of a guest. Now get out of here," said his father, "before I get the urge!"

Big John helped Dean unload the SUV. He was curious about the boxes. So, they sat at the dining room table in that little cabin drinking beer, just as Rafer and Dean had in the trailer in New Orleans, and just like Rafer had revealed to Dean what was in that world of boxes, Dean passed their history on to Big John.

He related how an idea had come on like some wildfire for an article or story about Giv, and how he had threaded his way through those people's lives. But it was also *their* lives, those American vignettes on existence. And Dean found himself going on about what he saw in Dallas and heard at the Oklahoma State Prison and it all seemed so . . .

He became this self-propelled talking machine, until he realized Big John was staring at those boxes as Dean had that first night in Rafer's trailer. "Sorry," said Dean. "It's been a long time since I . . ."

⁓

LATER THAT NIGHT Big John invited Dean to meet Randy's godfathers, who lived down at the trailer park on 94. He also wanted Dean to bring along Giv.

Riding down that hill with a case of beer and 750 milliliters of bourbon rattling away in the back, Big John explained about that trailer park.

It was exclusively for veterans. A married couple who had served in Vietnam had bought the park with one express idea—create a place for soldiers who had no place, who had been outnumbered, outmaneuvered and ultimately outgunned by human disregard.

Randy's godfathers were known as Bigote and Tortuga. Bigote had served with John Hernandez. Bigote means moustache. Tortuga means turtle. One had an immense moustache, and the other, to his dismay, was built like a turtle. These guys were divorced, Lipitor taking, liquor drinking, Diovan swallowing, hippie lettuce smoking, screw with-your-head, slightly-off-the-charts, sons of the republic.

Toward the rear of the park was a rec hall of sorts, which residents had built for themselves in '98. The hall was a styleless, cinderblock square shaded by California Peppers, but it had all the essentials—Jumbotron television, a working bar, tables to play cards, couches to kick back on, and an American flag that dominated one wall of photos of all those who had lived at the park and served their country.

When Big John arrived, Bigote and Tortuga were already

sitting at the bar, well into a healthy buzz. The place was otherwise empty. Big John did the intros. Bigote knelt down and shook Giv's paw. Then the boys got serious.

Bigote told Dean, "We're gonna have to do a search."

"I don't understand."

"A search," said Tortuga, "you know what a search is, don't you, Sergeant?"

"Yeah."

Dean glanced at Hernandez, who said only, "Policy."

Tortuga removed a pair of medical gloves from his back pocket. "A strip search for weapons, drugs."

"Excuse me," said Dean.

Bigote pointed to a small closet storage room behind the bar. Tortuga slipped on a medical glove and when he had it good and tight, snapped it.

Dean's voice caught in his throat. "I don't understand."

"Got to go in there and drop 'em."

"Excuse me?"

Tortuga got his other hand into a glove. "Come on, Sergeant, we got to do the whole runway."

"From taillights to headlights," said Bigote.

"Excuse me?"

"Get *him* done," said Bigote taking out his own pair of gloves. "I'll check the dog."

Bigote couldn't hold it together any longer. He just bundled up laughing, and Tortuga stomped one of those cloddy boots he wore into the cement floor. "Did you see his face?" Then Tortuga mocked Dean, "Excuse me . . ."

And Bigote chimed right in, pitching his voice up, "Excuse me?"

Tortuga took off the gloves and stuffed them down Dean's shirt.

⁓

NOW THEY GOT down to the serious business—seek out and destroy all remaining alcohol. Bigote was sprawled on the couch, letting Giv party on the foam from his head of beer.

"This is my kind of dog. Hard core. You hard core?" He sat up. He patted Giv and then took him by the muzzle and affectionately bit the dog on the head. Giv leapt up and put a lock on Bigote's forearm. Not enough to draw blood, just a little affectionate payback.

Bigote wobbled toward the bar with Giv still locked onto his forearm. Bigote had rounded that corner in his head where anything goes. He said to Dean who was at the bar with the others, "Did you know the army had dogs in Vietnam? In the jungle."

"Not tonight," said Tortuga.

"Dean's gonna write about a dog." Bigote pointed at Giv, then turned to Dean. "I'll tell you a story about dogs people should know." Bigote leaned against the bar. "The army took 'em to the jungles to scope out the Cong." He tapped his own nose with a beer. "In case Charlie was laying in wait. You know how many human lives those dogs saved? How many boys are here today because of them? Boys like me."

He pulled his arm up and Giv came with it and there the dog was. Bigote slid a beer Giv's way, and this got him to let go. "You know what the army did when the war ended?"

"Come on, Bigote," said Big John.

"They cut 'em loose. Dumped those dogs in the jungle. Dogs that had served this country. They cut 'em loose. They treated them just like they treated the returning soldiers. They cut 'em loose."

Tortuga grabbed Bigote's arm; Bigote yanked it free. "They treated those dogs like they treated all the soldiers. When the fighting's done, they cut 'em loose. Take a look now if you think it's any different. They should build a war memorial to those dogs. They should, 'cause they're heroes . . . just like *you* for serving . . . and *you* . . . and *Dean* and . . ."

"Our boy," said Big John.

Tortuga held up a beer. "Our boy."

Big John reached out with his beer, "Our boy."

Bigote followed suit with his beer. "Our boy."

And lastly Dean. "To a brother."

And so those beers all held together above the bar a long moment, for they were not only offering tribute to their own cherished lost child of the nation, but to all those men and women who were part of the mortal chain who had lit our way during war and darkness.

"And those dogs," said Bigote. "Them too, cause they're as much America as any of us."

They drank and Bigote served Giv more beer foam, and they toasted Giv with supraepithets for coming through his own suffering, and the men cried as men will who have had to deal with gravestones and the grievous tortures of the world.

And Dean, suddenly overwhelmed and defenseless against an accumulation of feelings, said to the men there, "I'm sorry."

They looked at him drunk and queerly and Tortuga asked, "For what? Trying to avoid a search?"

The men laughed but Dean said, "I didn't mean to survive. If I could go back and change places . . . I'm sorry . . . forgive me."

Big John grabbed the boy's hand with fierce resolve and held it flush upon the bar. "All of us here have been to that place, Sergeant. Let it go. You have that dog, you have those boxes, you have a dream. Honor the dead through your living."

"A-f——n' men," said Tortuga.

20

FINDING HOME

S EE GIV, SLIGHTLY wiped out, lying on his back, his legs upended, as Dean and Big John drove back to the house, drunk in any language. In that darkened yard John spoke to Dean without embellishment, "You need a home, son. A place you can lean on." John pointed to the cabin overhung as it was with trees.

Dean had no idea that night, the cabin, the scent of its wood on the softening warm air, the hints of sage and the cooling sandy earth, gave off an aura of another cabin in the west amidst the pooling light of the St. Peter's Truckstop sign, where Giv was born.

Giv, on the other hand, from the first, knew there was something. Dean saw it was that way with the dog. Dean would find him by the side of the house near a picnic table under a Palo Verde. He would sit there for endless hours and the contentment Dean saw there was enough to make him jealous.

What was it, Dean wondered? He, of course, could not know it was the smell of the cabin logs, and that sound the wind would make through the Palo Verde, like the one under which he had once slept, protected by his father's shadow in the garden above St. Peter's.

⁓

THE GET-EM game started simply enough the first time Dean and Giv hiked into the hills with Slip. The boy wanted to take them to Shepherd's Point. It was a local landmark of sorts in the Cleveland National Forest, about halfway between their house and Barrett Lake.

The Point had a grand view of the country, and someone had built an obelisk there, about fifteen feet high out of fieldstones. But this obelisk itself was not just an obelisk. It was a huge chimney with a single opening in the rock where you could make a fire. Hikers did, sightseers did, the beam of light it gave off could be seen going straight up into the sky from miles away. Though, in the last few years, because of the threat from wildfires, the opening had been cemented.

Who had built that obelisk or why, no one knew, nor how it got its name. Intriguing rumors abounded. There was only this plate-glass photo in a local museum of an old man with a wealth of beard and his white burro standing before that stone cairn.

There for the first time, Slip confessed to Dean that because of how he was born, he could never be a hero. It turned out his dream was to be Army like his father and brother, and Dean himself.

Dean had all kinds of answers to that notion of being a hero. Some were practical and intelligent, even inspired. At least one was cautionary, but children and their dreams are too inextricably linked to readily accept lessons of life and history.

It was also there that Slip asked, "If I take off running, you think Giv could catch me? But you got to give me a lead."

So the boy took off running while Dean held Giv, who was hungry to lay chase, especially with Slip yelling after him and finally when the boy had disappeared into the woods, Dean let Giv go and yelled, "Get-em."

Dean watched the dust powder under Giv's paws, and in no time after he hit those woods Slip yelled out. He'd been had. The game grew from there. A lead of thirty seconds became a minute, became two, became four. It did not matter. Giv tracked the kid up hills, across gullies, along forest slopes, with Dean following.

Now Slip hadn't earned his name for nothing and he worked out every trick. Once, he flung a shirt of his into a ravine then went off in the other direction. But Giv not only got the shirt, he lay chase with those raggy sleeves dangling from his mouth. Then he baited Slip into getting it back. He'd run a ways with the boy on his tail then Giv would drop down feigning exhaustion and when Slip got close, Giv would launch away.

Even when they were back at the house, Slip was still trying. He actually fell, or fake fell, and grabbed his ankle and cried out, and Giv just dropped down with the shirt soaked between his teeth, yards away, breathing heavily, but he did not go to the boy's rescue.

Dean and Big John watched from the picnic table by the cabin. Big John felt Giv had a bit of Bigote and Tortuga in him, the way he worked the boy's head, and he yelled to his son, "That dog knows BS when he sees it."

It did not take long for Dean to realize this was not just a game. The boy was trying to prove his mettle, that he could hike, run, hide, keep going in the heat. It was a matter of pride and strength and worthiness and durability and just being cool. Being "one of the guys."

At night Slip would sometimes open his bedroom window and shine his flashlight on the cabin, and Giv, who had become more like his own father and slept lying in sentry by the screen door, grew to know the signal and would head-butt open the door and join the boy.

They would hang in the dark under the Palo Verde and Slip would share the secrets of his private world in streams of imagination, without knowing Dean lay there in his bed listening.

There was an instance during one of those nights when Dean felt totally settled, completely calm and utterly connected to the world around him. There was only this symbiotic sweep of the mysterious substance that is life, and as he let himself totally immerse in it, just like that, it was gone, to be usurped by uncertainty and fear.

Was this a premonition of ill? Had the keen edge of his senses picked up on some nameless danger? Or was Dean Hickok still, Sergeant Dean Hickok of the U.S. Marines, who could not undo this knot within himself—that every good feeling would be short-lived no matter how long it went on.

The wars we fight, after the wars we fight. And yet, in the dark, alone, he had come to witness this precious calm and connection and even he understood—the moment and I have touched, which means it exists.

EVERY 4TH OF JULY there was a party at the trailer park that went on until the last man or woman standing. This 4th was to be no different. Outside the rec hall there were at least a dozen barbecues and smokers fired up, never mind that fifty-gallon half-drum with oak chips for all that tri-tip Big John meant to do Santa Margarita style. The air was dense with good eats and music and laughter and crazy talk, and Slip brought Dean door-to-door to meet anyone and everyone.

Now, Giv was not with Dean that morning. He had gone on an all-nighter with Bigote and Tortuga to San Diego. There was a DEA auction they wanted to hit. And besides that, Bigote's sister was driving down from L.A. to see him and meet Giv 'cause her brother had burned up endless AT&T minutes about "the dog and this soldier."

Their troop rumbled into the trailer park near noon in Tortuga's Silverado, his CD pounding the summer air with Grand Funk Railroad's "The Locomotion," telling everyone they had arrived. And man, had they.

Bigote was in the back of the pickup straddling something huge covered by a tarp. Giv was up front with Tortuga. Now, Bigote was wearing this high and square shako helmet from the War of 1812, and a Civil War Navy tunic that was a size too small and stank of mothballs. If that wasn't outrageous enough, his outfit was highlighted by a pair of American-flag Bermuda shorts and cowboy boots. The Silverado pulled up at the rec hall after doing a hard sweep and Tortuga jumped out.

Well . . . Tortuga was wearing a 16th century Italian casque helmet that swept down his head to the back of his shoulders, and a pair of British gauntlets. His fashion statement consisted of a t-shirt emblazoned with a skeleton wearing a top hat and smoking a cigar. Tortuga wore swimming trunks and flip-flops, and to be brutally honest, this gentleman did not have a body one would care to remotely envision in swimming trunks, unless one was turned on by uncooked turkeys.

Quite a crowd was gathering near the Silverado, and Giv jumped from the cab and started around the truck for Dean. *Why*, Dean wondered, *was the sun glinting off the dog's body?*

A breastplate of armor was strapped around his chest and back, that's why. The strips of metal were held together by this leather harness that banged and clanked, and when Giv leapt up to greet Dean, he nearly knocked him over. *This was a scene,* Dean thought, *that was in desperate need of Ruthie Ruth and her sketchpad.* But things were going to get a little stranger yet.

Tortuga took off in a jog down the road past the rec hall and he called to Slip 'cause he needed help, and Slip started off and when he did, Giv took off to join them clanking and banging.

People were asking Bigote what they had there under the tarp. Grinning wickedly, he said, "In a few minutes we are going to blow your mind."

Bigote then leaned over the side of the truck and corralled Dean. "Hey, I got something to tell you. Remember I said my sister and her husband were in L.A. on business, and she was gonna drive down to meet us in San Diego?"

"Yeah."

"Well, my sister is married to this wuss."

"Yeah."

"And the wuss's mother, well . . . she's pretty good considering all the miles on her odometer."

"Is there a point to this story?"

Big John now saw his son and Tortuga were dragging this old Port-A-San out from back where it lay dumped in the weeds, and they were setting it up at the end of the road. Big John yelled over to Bigote, "What the hell is he doing?"

"Of course, there is a point," said Bigote to Dean. "I told my sister all about you and the dog. And how you got hooked up and you being a Silver Star recipient. I told her about that girl in Katrina and the boy in prison. I told her you're writing a book, and she told the wuss, and the wuss called his mom, and his mom used to be some kind of editor for books and magazines and crap like that, and when she heard the story . . . She's interested and wants to talk to you about it. And that, my friend, *is* the friggin' point of the story."

Tortuga was jogging back to the Silverado with Slip and Giv in tow and yelling to Bigote, "We're ready," and Bigote was turning, when Dean got hold of his arm.

"Thanks." he said, "You have no idea what it means—"

"We stand together. That's why we're who we are. Now, let's rock."

Tortuga slid into the cab and got a CD going, and Giv leapt into the back, clanking and banging as Slip scrambled to join him, and Tortuga swung out of the cab and up into the truck bed.

As the music erupted, Bigote and Tortuga pulled away the tarp and there it was—a naval cannon. A black powder, 35-inch, naval-deck reenactor with a hardwood carriage. A pure cherry job if there ever was one. Bigote now proceeded to load it with powder and Tortuga lifted a cannonball they had stashed away. It turned out they had every intention of blowing that Port-A-San to kingdom come.

Now, this was the right kind of crowd for such insanity, especially when they had a few drinks under their belts, but discretion won out, and once that cannon was primed and loaded and aimed and ready, people were clearing back—way back. And Slip and Giv had to be forcibly removed from the truck bed.

Tortuga had spray painted rather large stick figures in a most ungracious pose on the Port-A-San wall. The boys let the music carry a little longer and then they "did" her. There was a violent boom. The cannon's whole carriage lurched back and hit the cab wall so hard it cracked the rear window. The cannonball was leaving a train of black smoke, but it had taken this nasty shank and was flying away from the target and toward the last house off to the right.

People watched in shock-and-awe, so to speak. And when it just cleared the roof of a double-wide there was this collective sigh until they heard one awful thud and a woman in the crowd, who was visiting, yelled out, "My car's back there."

⁓

DEAN WROTE DOWN everything about that day, from a cannonball leaving a smoky crater in the hood of a car, to when everyone gathered in the rec hall after dark for a moment of tribute and remembrance to the country.

Dean had been adopted that day by people's goodwill and he felt this overwhelming sense of humility.

He looked over at Giv, who sat watching into the night. Wearing that breastplate today, he had picked up the nickname Sir Perro Grande.

He called the dog over to where he sat on a porch chair and Giv rose up on his back legs and stretched across Dean's lap. Dean put out a hand and Giv parried with a lean muscled leg and Dean looked into that set of eyes, and that set of eyes, brightened by lamplight, looked back. The stare was immutable and never wavered. No distant constellation nor mere expression, but rather a touchstone to absolute camaraderie and affection, and Dean held that dog as he would his dearest friends destroyed or dead around him on the Euphrates. *Kinship*, thought Dean, *that's what this is, pure kinship.*

[21]

INFERNO

I T WAS A meager patch of brush that Slip saw from Shepherd's Point, in a nothing gully smoldering with small match tips of flame. Just candle rows in a church, no more. The opportune wind bending and turning the flames like helpless children.

The weather in the west that summer was a war zone of heat and drought. A natural malediction turning scrub into a wreath of death through the slightest mishap. Common sense should have told Slip to get back home to protect himself.

But within was a need to validate himself, to confront some adversary, and prove worthy of men's respect. The desire for valor, immense and demanding, and the fire out there, so very small.

He crabbed his way down the incline. It was three hundred

yards through harsh and waterless brush. By the time he reached the fire it was a small pocket that covered yards. He took off his shirt and beat at the flames; he grabbed handfuls of dirt to smother them.

He was drenched in sweat and his face flushed red from the heat and sun. Soon the ground around him was just a smoldering remnant of an almost-fire that he kept heaping dirt upon to suffocate, when a sound caught his ear like the great whoosh of a train through a hollow of track. What he heard turned his head, and then what he saw was a wall of fire spilling out in veins along the ridgeline, fierce and windswept and utterly unstoppable.

DEAN WAS IN Los Angeles visiting the Chaplain who had been there for him in the hospital when he got a call from Big John. There was a fire; houses were being evacuated. At this point John did not know his son was somewhere in those hills and it would be two crucial hours before he even suspected.

Dean had pushed it all the way but when he reached 94 he drove at a punishing pace. Past Indian Springs, above the mountains to the southeast, were the first signs of havoc poisoning the sky. When he reached Barrett Junction a disaster was upon them. A mushroom cloud of smoke, tongues of flame along the hilltops, huge now and snapping virulently and turning the crestline into the mouth of some dark netherworld.

By the Barrett Junction Café, volunteer firefighters were assembling up for their trek into the hills. Small platoons of them were already crossing the road, hunchbacked with equipment. There were firetrucks and news vans and locals with their packed trucks and horse trailers. He searched for Big John and Slip. He called their cell but couldn't get through. He sped on to the trailer park and up Hermosita where firefighters moved in lines through the day, their picks and shovels clanging, and dust rising from their boots. When Dean swung into the turnoff he was flagged to a stop by sheriffs.

Just ahead, fire trucks in a half moon tried to lace the flames with high-powered hoses. The road near gone in the black of smoke. The wind tousled the choking draft this way and that. And flames, wild braids of them, were taking out brush all the way up the incline while the sheriff's department kept Hermosita closed to anything incoming.

When Dean was swinging the SUV around to go back to the trailer park, he spotted Big John by a patrol car. He was confronting the sheriffs, while Bigote and Tortuga were this wall of profanity backing him up.

Dean got out of the car calling to the boys and they tumbled over each other trying to explain how Slip was lost, that he'd been at the Barrett Junction Café that morning, then was last spotted by a neighbor trekking it into the hills. Search-and-Rescue had been alerted. Police and news choppers were notified.

Big John had no intention of remaining back with the

others behind the fire line. The sheriffs knew him well and were doing everything they could to keep from cuffing him, but he was a beast of a man in the midst of dread trying to find his son.

Dean understood it would be hopeless if John went into those hills. He never hiked; he'd end up a lost casualty. The sheriffs now were putting it to him with their own special brand of religion, short of an arrest. They ordered him down on his knees. Dean glanced at Giv there in the shotgun seat, his head protruding from the window, alert and clipping from side to side, calling out.

The moment descends as only the naked possibility of death can, headlong and enormous, and Dean was there again on the Euphrates, within the circle of fire and men around a Humvee like shipwrecked victims near the corpse of their boat. They are the pictures of life forever left upon the wilderness of his soul. And their blood—he can see it pooling in the sand like the petals of a broken rose, and the need to act obliterates all else.

Dean looked back to where the road had been cordoned off. He grabbed Bigote who was closer. He called to Tortuga amidst the passing line of the firefighters.

"I want you to go up there," said Dean, "and those men, those sheriffs, get them away from the road."

They did not understand.

"So I can get through."

They were crowded in together and their expressions, breathed with confusion.

"Do you understand? I'll get him home. Giv will find him. Now go . . . Go!"

They ran up the road as Dean got into the SUV. He leaned over and grabbed the seatbelt and got Giv strapped in as best he could. "Stay right there, please. Stay." He pressed his hand against the dog's chest. "Just stay."

Bigote and Tortuga were talking out a plan as they ambled past the firetrucks, and when they got within yards of the sheriffs, they took off toward the shoulder as if they meant to get around the roadblock. The sheriffs spotted them and yelled out to stop, but Bigote and Tortuga kept running and the sheriffs took the bait and went after them.

Dean shifted into first. In America there is a state of being we all carry in our blood. We were born from it and we will die with it, because of it, or in spite of it. It's being pure rebel. It's as indigenous to us as natural law. We worship it as much as the tattered flag that traces our name. Being pure rebel. Right or wrong. Just go. And keep the rest where it belongs, in your rearview mirror. Dean hit the gas.

The SUV kicked it past lines of shovel-and-pick fire-fighters and sped into the road with the flames and firetrucks and rising smoke and went right past the sheriff's car where the road sloughed through a charred and smoldering landscape. He rode the horn past a collection of stunned onlookers shuttling back and out of his way shouting for him to stop, but he kept right on past more sheriff cars and firetrucks and a great wall of water from the giant hoses that drenched his car and he was past them all in one willful expression of defiance.

Halfway up Hermosita the road cleared and Dean went first for the house on the chance Slip might have managed to reach there. As the SUV swung into the front yard, a newschopper cut across the sky overhead, and by the time it had arced around Dean was swerving out of the driveway and up Hermosita again.

There was a dirt road about a half-mile away that took you pretty close to Shepherd's Point, but it meant going through the heart of the fire. He was being followed from above now, and as he rumbled onto that dirt road a police helicopter appeared out of the white-hot distance aiming right for him.

The road descended hard and rutted through a wild landscape of mesquite spotted with burns, and the helicopters were right on him as the road rose up through a rocky crag. When he reached the top, just right there, he had to hit the brakes so hard the SUV jerked sideways and the rear panel was gored by rock and ripped clean through.

The sun glistened across the windshield and Dean could take in all that awful breadth of carnage. Waves of fire were moving against the hills in a sheering wind. A sea of torched black slope, the only remains rough pockets of rock reminiscent of burial mounds. And the smoke rising like some colossus, foul and grey.

But it was that stretch a quarter mile ahead Dean watched, nearly hypnotized, where the fire had devoured the ground on both sides of the camino for what looked to be about a hundred yards. Sometimes he could see that ribbon of earth running straight as an arrow down the center of that carnage like the parting of the Red Sea. Then the wind crazed the flames and they would suck back in on themselves and the road was consumed.

There was no getting past that. There was only going through it. If it could be done, well, farther on there was smoke, but the road looked serviceable.

The police helicopter was directly overhead and a voice on a loudspeaker was calling down to him, ordering, demanding he turn back. The news chopper was off to his left filming.

He grabbed the edge of his t-shirt sleeve and wiped the sweat and ash from his eyes. He looked over at Giv who was panting heavily. He closed the electric windows. Turned up the air conditioner so the inside of the car became like ice. He reached into the back for his Marine duffel. He emptied it of his clothes. He grabbed two jugs of water from the floor. The first he put in the duffel. He poured water from the second into his hands for Giv to drink till he was sated. Then Dean gulped down as much water as he could stand. He got out of the car and doused the windshield to clear away the dirt. The voice kept coming down on him from above to go back—for his own safety, just go back. He climbed into the SUV and closed the door. He stuffed the second jug into that duffel. He looked at Giv who now stared on toward the fire. Dean gripped the wheel hard, then faced the road ahead.

You are never alone, even when you most believe you are. You are never alone, because those who have left you are never truly gone. They are with you now. Ruthie Ruth and Ian . . . Giv's father . . . all the souls in that garden above St. Peter's or who were felled along the banks of the Euphrates. They are the linchpins sunk into the earth who will guide you. They are whispering to you now as you shift into gear and begin the run.

The road was brutal but he picked up speed. The speedometer rose and the shocks rattled violently as they rushed toward the yawing mouth of a fire waiting to swallow them whole.

Dean could see the water streaks across the windshield begin to heat and crackle and break down into mere beads that tremored on the glass as they boiled and then burst apart.

The SUV was there and then it was gone. Into the fire. The flames leapt up over the engine hood and crushed against the windshield. The world was consumed. Flames streaked along the windows.

The SUV seemed to draw in the air and the fire responded in wicked assault. Dean could hear it slapping against the glass by his face. Great pools of it. The vehicle was shuddering. Just feet of road ahead. That's where he kept his eyes, watching over the hood where tiny bullets of paint began to blister up. And his window—he didn't see, wouldn't look, but could hear. Tiny spider cracks were making their way up through the glass.

The heat was closing in along the body of that SUV. Along the door panel. The roof above his head. He could feel it pressing against the bottoms of his boots. His hands were bloodless white, and whiter yet against the fierce sheen of the flames. Even Giv could feel the heat and bent away from the door. The inside of that rig grew hotter by the second. Bits of paint were spit against the windshield.

And then a tire blew.

The truck swerved, then dipped as the ground gave way and it took all Dean had to keep them from tilting over. Suddenly the earth rose and there was this horrid scoring where the wheel rim sparked rock, and they were in mid-air when that wall of fire just whooshed apart and they slammed back down in a surge of daylight, the truck rocking, listing, one shock breaking apart, the fan severing, then gashing through the radiator as the truck caromed into a declination of sand then came to a ferocious stop.

A stunned Dean wiped a closed fist across his forehead as the engine burned, and then he staggered out of the truck. Giv had come partway through the seat belt and was trapped upside down wriggling, till Dean got him loose.

Dean grabbed the duffel and looked the truck over. It was finished. Getting Slip out now would have to be done on foot. He looked up for the helicopters, but there was too much ground smoke for them to be seen.

He took off running. "Come on," he yelled and Giv sprinted up alongside him.

There was a narrow arroyo whose slopes they'd hiked

endless times, that was now a river of smoke until they reached the top, and on the other side, upon a slant of open ground, stood the obelisk.

It was there that Dean knelt and took out the jug of water for Giv to drink again. He wet down the dog's face and then he drank himself. He put the jug back and took hold of Giv by the sides of his neck and in utter desperation said, "Get 'em . . . Go!"

For a moment the dog just blinked and stared, and Dean said again with even more urgency, "Get 'em . . . Get 'em!"

The dog's ears went back and he took to the ground.

Head low, neck stretched out, Giv was like a divining rod moving about the obelisk then trailing off. The spreading gully was a spectacle of untouched brush cut by seared pathways of devastation that still smoldered or burned.

The dog made his way into this labyrinth, first in one direction and then another, skirting the cremated remains of trees, hesitating, turning back, putting his nose to the air, coming about and starting again. Then he quickly jumped an entangled mass of undergrowth, his head rising into a wind of frayed traces, with Dean following all the while.

It seemed to Dean the dog was unsure and left to chasing ghostly scents, when in fact, he was tracking the panicked confusions of a child who had started in one direction then veered off, who had hidden behind huge rocks against an onslaught of fire, and who had made his way choking into a deepening maze of trees where weaves of smoke drifted among the branches. Far ahead of the dog, in a slip of light upon the hillside, was a foreboding mark upon the earth.

Giv reached the boy well ahead of Dean. He circled and barked, and he leaned down low pushing at Slip with his head, trying to rouse him. Dean rushed up and skidded to his knees beside the boy. He saw right off Slip was still breathing, that his pants legs were singed but he was not burned. Dean called out to him as he checked to find wounds, then he rolled the boy's eyelids back and they fluttered a bit. He wet the boy's face; he even tried to get some water into his mouth, but Slip just lay there unconscious.

Dean tried his cell but knew already it would be dead. There was little left to consider except where the winds would take the fire.

Giv was still trying to rouse Slip by prodding at him with his muzzle, and making these sharp hurting breaths.

He hugged Giv and said, "You got him . . . You got him."

Dean tossed the near-empty jug from the duffel; the other he opened and tried to get Giv to drink but he would not, he was too intent. Dean again swallowed as much water as he could handle. He wet his head and he ran some over Slip's face. He lifted the boy's legs and slid the duffel under them shimmying it slowly up the boy's body. It would reach nearly up to Slip's chest. Then Dean looped the canvas strap over his shoulder and he lifted.

Dean stood and Giv stood. *I have carried this much weight,* thought Dean, *from boot camp to battlefields.* They began their march over terrain that crackled with sparks, he and the dog, side by side. Dean was trying to compass away from the wind and fires, but in truth, he was hoping a chopper would be cutting sky over this wilderness and find them.

They struggled down a long ravine of littered rock. The wind had intensified and sparks of fire were being carried over the ridgetop. They began the climb up a gravelly slope, and this is where Giv began to veer away from Dean.

Dean halted there and called to the dog, but Giv kept on running for yards, then stopped and looked back. The incline was steeper there, much more difficult, and the canvas strap had already cut into Dean's shoulder and blood was seeping down his chest.

The dog continued on up and turned, and by then Dean was following him, trying to scrabble his way up through all that loose gravel. Reaching a plate of ground to rest a moment and get a breath in all that smoke, he saw where he had been going, the fire now was. The wind was kicking up foul licks that snapped and spired and then came apart in the air, casting more burning flecks upon the sky.

The landscape ahead was a smoky delirium impossible to see through and gain bearing or direction. They descended what seemed like miles over ground that was flinty and rutted, the dog always a few steps ahead.

Dean began to break down. The pain in his shoulder a pure knife blade as the strap cut deep into muscle. His legs were giving way, and he listed from one side to the other.

Suddenly he realized that Giv was gone. He looked

about calling, keeping on, and then there he was again, a specter in the haze standing at the edge of a culvert.

As he caught up to Giv, Dean dropped down to his knees. Had the dog led them here? He put his arm around Giv. Dean knew this open culvert; it stretched a mile up to the lake. He and the boy and the dog had traversed it many times. There was water tumbling down through that channel, and if they could get across that ten-foot spanse of concrete, then straight on through the wilderness would be a pair of fieldstone pillars that flanked a main pathway into the National Forest. A dirt parking lot was just beyond those pillars, and it would be a logical place for firefighters and trucks to gather up together.

Ten hard feet was all. He tried to ease down into the causeway, but the pull of the water was far too dangerous while he had the boy. He could see a few dozen yards into the smoke. In one direction there was an incline, steep and suspect. He took the other, having remembered there were stanchions embedded into the concrete channel where wire mesh had been strung to act as a kind of grate. There, he could make a crossing.

It took precious time to find a set of stanchions, but there was no wire mesh and that would make the crossing all that more treacherous. Dean eased his way into the water with tremendous care, telling Giv to stay back, stay, wait. The machinery of Dean's muscles was grinding down. He stretched toward the stanchion, and when he had it in hand, he pulled. The current was near chest high and almost dragged him loose. He reached for the next stanchion, and he and Slip went under momentarily. He came up gasping and steadied himself, and then he grasped the steel rod and in one fevered lunge made the edge of the culvert and clawed his way up onto the dirt.

Dean yelled to Giv, "Come on . . . Come on." He had seen the dog make the jump before, and Giv paced back and forth along the edge of the culvert, his head raised, snapping at the air, and Dean pounded the ground again. "Come on . . . !"

Dean put out his hands and Giv hunched down and rose up and sniffed at the culvert, and then he muscled back and edged around and Dean yelled through the smoke, "Come on . . ." and he slapped his hands together. Giv's ears set and his jaw muscles tightened and he sprinted forward and leapt.

He covered the distance in one long extended stretch and his image friezed across that rumbling face of water.

But he fell short. Giv hit the culvert wall and his leg bone broke above the paw. He cried out and tumbled into the current and Dean barely got a hold of him by the skin above his neck before he could be flooded away.

Giv tumbled over and he looked up at Dean, water pouring over his head, trying desperately to breathe. Dean looked down at Giv and the dog stared up at him half buried in the current.

His look knew the limits of the earth were upon them; and Dean, he knew Giv was the journey—he was all those miles. He was kinship, friend, anchor, part of the enormous roots of the world that demanded his will, and he tried to pull, he tried to lift Giv from the water. He tried to keep from going in himself. He tried, and he tried, but he could not hold. His strength was broken, and Giv tumbled away down through the culvert and into the smoke and was gone.

⁓

THE FIRST SIGHTINGS from the air were thought to be a mirage, something the smoke had tricked out. News trucks and sheriff's cars raced to the scene as rumor rose to the level of reality. They all waited in the sandy lot just outside the National Forest—Big John, Bigote and Tortuga, emotionally spent even at praying.

There were helicopters working the sky when someone yelled, "There." No one knew who that was, but where light coursed through the smoke and across those fieldstone pillars a figure emerged with a duffel slung across his chest.

By the time they reached Dean, he was staggering, then downed. When they removed the duffel, the strap had stolen about an inch of flesh from his muscle.

He cried out as he fell, "I've got to go back. He's up there. He has a broken leg."

While they prepared to rush Dean away in an ambulance he grabbed Big John's hand. "It wasn't me. It was him. We can't leave him there to die."

He could hear the words through his own haze, but they were just sound with shadows.

22

"ANGEL, WE'VE FOUND OUR BOY"

D OGS OF EVERY KIND, *every shape and size—
ancient dogs, cartoon dogs, famous dogs, futuristic
dogs, hipster dogs, movie dogs, mythological dogs,
Norman Rockwell dogs, ridiculously funny dogs—each is a visual
fabrication on a fragment of cloth that has been quilted together
from remnants to make a spread that covers the couch in the office
at St. Peter's.*

*Angel is the grand matron now, preeminent and breathing
heavily, and her place on the couch includes the armrest nearest
Anna. There are three other dogs at St. Peter's, the royal court as
Anna calls them, from that legion of the lost and wounded. The
rest of the couch belongs to them.*

*Three years has done little to lessen Anna's sorrow at losing
Giv. Every day brings a new prayer for his well-being. On the
bulletin board, between that photograph the soldier took and the*

pawn ticket, is a snapshot of Giv sunning himself—just pure puppy. He is Anna's rose of the earth, her celestial blood.

And there were nights, especially when it was dangerously warm and dry, and the wind rustled through the arteries of the Palo Verde that Anna heard Giv's voice saying . . . *I am here, mother . . . I am here . . . I am still walking this side of eternity and have never forgotten your love . . .*

It was on such a night, sitting outside her bungalow and drinking a beer, with only the television on in that tiny living room, that she picked up snippets of news. A fire in California . . . a horrific tempest of flames . . . a young man . . . a soldier with a dog . . . entered the inferno to save a boy's life.

Anna found herself leaning toward the open door till the television came into view. Framed there in the dark, the fire was shown from a sweeping chopper, over hills scorched and smoking between banded runs of flame. The chopper rose on the thermals, shaking precariously to clear another rise, and the earth opened again into endless apocalyptic destruction.

A reporter explained what Anna was seeing. A hillside breathing fire. The strange contour of trees turned into immense burned stalks. And out of this a figure appeared, imperiled and half-staggering. It was the soldier.

His clothes had been touched by fire: his face was singed and sooted. Slung from one shoulder his Marine duffel. The strap had dug so deep into the muscles the blood formed a baldric across his chest. In the duffel, head and arm hanging out, the unconscious boy.

They said the soldier's name . . . and the dog's. "The dog . . . was missing and presumed dead." Had Anna heard right? It came so fast. She was kneeling by the television in the dark now . . . Had she heard right?

She hung on every word, every image. They did not repeat the dog's name. They showed footage of the SUV filmed from high above hurtling forward on what was at best a fire road, toward a world of flames.

Reporters on site filled in the story, but they did not repeat the dog's name, only that he was missing and presumed dead and it was he who'd found the boy.

Anna was a creature beset with one question and they cut away. She slammed the television and the dogs lying asleep on the bed shot up. Now it was another reporter with her tweaked hair and too-white teeth. Only this one had "exclusive footage."

A huge American flag had been strung between two trees. Smoke from char grills filled the air. There was music. It was the usual shaky home camera footage of pleasant mundanities. Then they were by a picnic table beneath a Palo Verde caught in a moment unawares.

Sergeant Dean Hickok, late of the U.S. Marines, and Giv. With the first sight of Giv she could hear the air gust out of her. The dog was standing on his hind legs, the front paws against the soldier's chest. Dean had got hold of both sides of Giv's muzzle and was grappling him affectionately.

The son had grown to be the father. Years were swept

aside instantly. They were like nothing now but a fictional abyss that never happened.

"Angel," Anna whispered. "We've found our boy."

Of course, it could all be coincidence and that dog was not her Giv, but by dawn Anna was driving to California in her ratty old pickup. She had with her the snapshot of Giv, the father's collar, and the pawn ticket.

Dean Hickok was in a La Mesa, California hospital. When Anna pulled into the parking lot, there was a lineup of news trucks. She walked among the reporters as they rehearsed for on-camera spots. It was a virtual bio in short bursts of Hickok and Giv. The war hero with the Silver Star, and the dog he'd found left for dead on a Kentucky road at night in the rain. How the soldier tried to find the girl in New Orleans who Giv belonged with—a victim of Katrina who died trying to save another animal during the flood. And how it was ultimately the dog who had led the way through that ash wasteland, proving man and dog were truly inseparable.

Anna had come to California with no plan in mind about how to meet Dean Hickok. She was in the hospital commissary having coffee, when who should walk in but the boy's father?

She'd seen John Hernandez being interviewed on the cable shows. He was with a small coterie of tough-looking characters. The boots were a thick-as-blood crowd. Veterans with map-lined faces sat around Hernandez. Occasionally a passerby would offer a hello or wish Hernandez well.

But when that photo of Giv's father and Angel was

placed on the table before him, Hernandez was caught completely on his heels. He looked up at this woman with sunglasses and wild hair. "What is this?"

"This," said Anna, pointing at the photo, "is Giv's father. And this is Angel, Giv's mother."

Bigote took the photo and spun it around for the others to get a look-see. Anna took the snapshot of Giv and put that on the table. "This is Giv. I named him after his father."

"You named him?"

"Giv was stolen from me when he was a puppy."

Tortuga glanced from the photo to the woman, and said, "The crackpots have arrived."

Anna glared at the man.

"Get out of here, lady," said Bigote. "Whatever you're trying to sell, do, exploit, we're not interested."

"I have only one interest. Finding Giv."

Big John was still pretty much locked into the photos. He had them side by side. The resemblance was impossible to deny.

"Mr. Hernandez," said Anna. "If I could just talk to the Sergeant for a few minutes. Long enough for him to show me where on a map, explain the place to me, so I could get close enough to where he lost Giv. I would go up there now. And try to find him."

Big John looked up suspiciously and asked, "If you found him, what then?"

"I'd bring him to the sergeant, of course." She looked about the table as if the answer would be plainly obvious.

"But, if Giv were dead, and I found the body . . ." her mouth opened to get more air . . . "I'd ask the sergeant if I might bury Giv with his father. His father is buried under that tree." She put her hand on the Palo Verde in the photograph. "There. I buried *him* in the place he loved most. On the hill behind a truck stop I own. St. Peter's."

Hernandez saw her hand linger on the photo. He could see in the hand—the way it moved, the way it just felt the paper—the physicality of loss. He had seen it in his own hands when he'd taken the flag from the color guard at his son's funeral. The inanimate object—you touch it because it is the closest you will ever be to a loved one again in this lifetime.

Anna picked up the photos and placed them carefully in a folder. She excused herself and apologized. She told Mr. Hernandez, "I'll be here. In this commissary, or the lobby. I'll give you my cell phone number." She had written it down on a St. Peter's business card. She set that down on the table and apologized again.

The men at the table were of two camps. The woman was either a flake or the sad exploiter of an uncanny resemblance. But there was also something Big John knew that the others did not. Dean had confided to him once that Giv had, in fact, been stolen.

⁓

MR. HERNANDEZ APPROACHED her table. He was looking her business card over. He leaned down and rested his hands on the back of the chair facing her.

"Your name is Anna?"

"Yes."

"St. Peter's Truck Stop?"

"It's a small motel really. That's what's left."

"What makes you think you could find Giv up there?"

"Well, I have a talent. Affliction might actually be a better word for it, that makes me eminently suited to find him. If anyone can find him."

She saw Hernandez's eyes begin to redden and shield over with tears. "Let's talk."

DEAN LAY ASLEEP. He had on a mask for oxygen. Surgery had been performed to repair shoulder muscles that were akin to shredded tire rubber. The doctors told Dean he would never be able to raise that arm above his shoulder. The burns had been negligible, but his lungs had taken a severe hit of smoke and heated ash. His throat was no better. He could barely piece together two words, and what he could, sounded as if they were coming up through miles of sanded gravel.

When his eyelids finally fluttered enough for the light to get in, the first he saw through that groggy haze was a woman wearing sunglasses, sitting near the window.

"Hello," she said.

He tried to get out the word, "Who . . ."

"Her name is Anna," said John.

He came around the bed and pulled up a chair so he

could be close to Dean. "Listen, son, this woman feels she might be able to help find Giv, and she's willing to go up into the fire zone and face the risk. She wants you to show her on a map where you lost him. As close as you can get." Big John reached for a folder on the bedstand. "I wouldn't go along with this unless . . . well, she *claims* Giv was stolen from her."

Dean's eyes moved from Big John to Anna. Big John opened the file to show Dean the photos. Anna watched as the sergeant's emotions pieced together. He tried to speak but the words broke down in his throat. He motioned for a pen to write with. Anna took one from her shoulder bag. He wrote on the folder—*Prove to me what you say.*

And prove it she did. She told him about St. Peter's and how two musicians arrived. Brothers. One named Jem and the other—

23

PRAYING FOR YOU
TO COME HOME

DEAN HAD NO intention of showing Anna on a map where he'd lost Giv, but he did have every intention of taking her there himself, or fall trying.

Dean knew the doctors wouldn't release him, and that Big John and the others would prevent him from going, out of concern for his health. So, Dean asked if he could have a few minutes with Anna alone. He then removed the oxygen mask to see how tough breathing would be, and how he might cope with that ashen fire zone. He tried to speak but the words just kept breaking down so he wrote—*Find a stairwell away from the newstrucks where you can park your car, then come back and help me get away without being seen.*

She reminded him he couldn't even sit up, and how did he plan to deal with his arm? He wrote—*I'll deal with it.*

On the way out, Dean went to Slip's room. He lay there alone and asleep. Dean woke him gently. The boy was still weak but when he saw Dean dressed and his arm in a make-shift sling he sat up, shocked and staring, "What . . . ?"

Dean put a finger to his lips and handed the boy a note— *I'm going back for Giv.*

Slip grabbed Dean's arm, "I'm sorry for what I caused . . . Do you think he'll forgive me?"

WHILE ANNA DROVE, Dean tried to rest through the pain. She'd rigged up a sort of sling with his hospital bedsheet. The wind coming in the open window cooled his burns but every breath was its own telltale war.

They had one stop to make before trekking into the hills. Anna needed something with Giv's scent on it. The Sheriff's department had opened Hermosita to traffic, and Anna followed Dean to the rear of Hernandez's darkened home and into the tiny guest apartment. While Dean tried to decide what would best have Giv's scent on it, she walked right over to a wide-bodied corduroy chair with a souvenir shop pillow.

All Dean could do was watch in amazement as she said, "This is his area, right? His chair." She picked up the pil-low and held it close to her face. "This will do."

The pillowcase didn't come off so she asked for a knife and cut the fabric from one side of it.

Before they got back into her truck, Dean decided now it would be all right to call Big John. As Dean could hardly speak, he handed the phone to Anna. "Mr. Hernandez, we're going into the hills."

"I suspected as much," he said, "The newspeople . . . they know Dean's gone, and they're all over the map. Take care of my boy, will you?"

From there on, it was a dirt road to the ink-washed distance, till finally, Dean pointed. They had arrived at the remains of the gate. The headlights fleshed it out right down to the seams of those fieldstone columns. But there was something else.

Dean managed, "Headlights . . . Keep on." Just getting out of the truck his legs buckled, and the pain moving through his shoulder and into his chest turned him ashen white, and he thought he would pass out.

All around the base of those columns and along the entrance to the pathway, people had left flowers and cards and picturebooks and votive candles and handwritten letters from both adults and children. They were held in place on the ground by stones and their edges fluttered as if they were alive. Anna knelt and took up a card and then stood and angled it so she could use the headlights to read it aloud.

It was to Giv—*We are all proud of you and we are praying that you come home safely*. It was signed by every child in the second grade class at El Cajon elementary.

This outpouring of emotion nearly overwhelmed Dean.

It took a few hard breaths to keep himself in check for what was ahead. She put the card back, then Dean pointed far up into the blackness where smoke drifted across the moonless crest.

Anna went around to the back of the truck. In the bed was a utility box that she unlocked. She called Dean over. She took out the carryall and started to fill it. First with a flare gun, then a bullhorn to call to Giv. There were canteens and extra water and goggles and a first aid kit—since they knew Giv had at least a broken leg. Then she took out a holstered revolver. "In case we need to scare something off . . . Why don't you carry it?"

Dean took the gun and clipped the holster to his belt. He managed one word . . . "Prepared."

"I've been on searches before."

She grabbed a handful of breathing masks and dumped them into the carryall. One she slipped around Dean's neck.

"My late husband was a soldier," she said. "He died when he was about your age. You'd have been his kind of guy." She touched the side of Dean's face.

Lastly, she took out a portable HID and extra battery mags. The extra mags she dumped into the carryall; the searchlight she handed to Dean. "Military grade," she said.

He aimed and flicked the on-switch. A tunnel of light shot past the gate and up the hillside for hundreds of yards.

"Lead the way, Sergeant," she said.

UP THROUGH THAT smoldering hillface they went. Along the promontory uncertain vestiges beyond the smoke, like faintly breathing shadows. Dean led Anna to a pitched crepe of rock. From there, he pointed the light down the ravine face. There was a slender gulf of land that ran through the hills.

"The road," said Dean, ". . . there."

The ground along the road resembled some hideous blackened hide, and the burned trees made this gruesome moan in the slightest wind. There were some spots of fire along the slopes, but beyond a far ridgetip there was a deep pulsing where flames still raged.

The road led them to the scorched remains of Dean's SUV. The light flooded across the hull. It sat at an angle in the sloping dust up to its wheelwells. Smoke drifted through the glassless windows and the hollows where the headlights had been. Anna stopped short when she first saw the SUV not realizing what it was.

Dean aimed the light back down the road where he and Giv had run the fire. *If we could come through that . . .* , he thought. He traced the light on into the hills. They were maybe a half-mile from where he'd lost Giv.

He walked over and touched Anna's shoulder. She had been staring at the truck. She'd seen it run the flames on the news, but this close to the wreckage brought about the most stark invasion of thoughts.

She turned. Dean pointed the light up through a shallow arroyo to a craggy incline. "Half mile . . . lost Giv . . ." He poked a finger down toward the ground where they stood, ". . . Till light."

So here they would wait. Dean ran the searchlight over the truck and paced it with quiet regard. In the sand around the base were spidery runs of silver that stood out luminously. Dean knelt by one and had Anna come over. He reached into the sand and carefully pulled one loose. He handed the hardened metallic rivulet to her. She did not understand.

"Chrome . . . so hot . . . melted."

She held it as if it were some tiny lightning bolt fallen from the heavens.

There was a large, half-buried rock by the side of the road near the truck, where Dean sat uncertainly in the sand, trying to find some means to be comfortable with all that pain. Anna brought him over a canteen, and he drank, and she sat on the rock beside him in the dark.

He did not notice she had taken from her pocket the pawn ticket in its plastic casing and was holding it as one might in prayer.

"When we find him," she said, "there is something I want."

Dean looked up at her.

"If he's alive, he stays with you. It couldn't be any other way now. But . . . if he's not, I'd like to take him home and bury him with his father."

Dean had seen the photo and been told the tale. He agreed with a nod.

"There is something else," she said, "if he is alive, that I want."

Dean studied Anna closely.

"I'd like you to arrange, or we could arrange it together, that Giv have . . . a litter sometime, and . . . you might let me have a son of his. It would mean very much to me."

Her voice was scarcely above a whisper when she asked; and in that moment, Dean Hickok, late of the U.S. Marines, and Anna Perenna, were utterly connected, as only two people can who have endured immense catastrophes.

He reached out and took her hand as a way to tell her—yes. It was then that he noticed she was holding something wrapped in plastic.

Curious, he turned the light on it. It was two halves of a pawn ticket.

She told him about the collar and the watch repairman and how Giv got his name and the pawn ticket discovered inside the casing, and how she had tried to find the shop, but it no longer existed, so now she would never know.

Dean had been holding the ticket closely while she spoke, looking it over, especially where that cut line went through the address. The paper was badly frayed, but something caught his attention. Maybe because it tapped into that summer he and his sister stood on the banks of the Mississippi in East St. Louis.

Dean scratched out a few words, ". . . East St. Louis."

"I don't understand."

"Did you . . . try?"

"I tried St. Louis."

Dean pointed at Anna. "Budapest."

"That's right. That's where I'm from."

"Buda . . . city. Pest . . ."

"Budapest, yes. On one side of the river is Buda and the other—"

"East St. Louis . . . Illinois . . ."

She had not even known there was an East St. Louis, let alone across the river in Illinois. And in all that time no one—

She stood suddenly, alert now to the dark.

"What?" asked Dean.

She took a few steps reckoning. Her garments moved slightly with the wind. "There's something out there," she said.

Dean slowly stood; he was on guard now. He turned the searchlight upon that wasteland. Hillocks of sand and ravaged brush—it was quiet as death out there.

"No," said Anna. "Put the light there."

She was pointing to where the road slipped off into the canyon.

24

LEAPING THE ABYSS

THE WOLF WATCHED, crouched and wary, from that dry river bottom of a road. He was not alone. A pack of his fellow travelers rushed past, their eyes hot as burning meteors.

Dean tried to trail them with the searchlight, but they negotiated the terrain all too nimbly. One thing was certain. "They're circling," said Anna.

Dean took Anna by the arm and got her quickly to the SUV where there was a cratered space along one side that backed up to the hull. He made Anna kneel down there.

"Carryall," he said.

He squatted beside her. He opened the carryall and skimmed through it. He considered using the flares to scare them off, but he thought they might kindle up more brushfires.

There wasn't much. The bullhorn. Well . . . He took it from the carryall and set it in the sand on the crater ledge. He undid the holster at his side and placed the gun by the bullhorn.

Then, Anna saw the wolves. They were loping quickly through the dark, kicking up spots of dust. They were closer now.

"I can see them," she said.

Using his good arm, Dean slipped the other out of the sling and cast the sling away. As he let the bad arm down that whole side was so riven with pain, he had to rest his head against the blistered paneling until it passed.

Another wolf sprinted by the vehicle, testing the air, then rushing away.

"Keep . . . the light . . . on 'em."

Anna did as she was asked. She held the light high and trained it on the ground before them, panning from side to side. Dean took the bullhorn in one hand, the pistol in the other and stood. He undid the safety.

One of their kind rushed the dark again, the long flue of the muzzle showing teeth, and Dean put the gun barrel across the mouthpiece of the bullhorn and fired off a delinquent shot at the horizon.

The concussion of the shot resounded through the bullhorn against that reef of hills and the lobo came straight off the ground with legs stiff as a corpse. He twisted in the air, then took off like a dervish for the dark.

The rest of that black and wild pack hovered at the edge

of the light, unsure, retreating, crouching, tailing back, defiant, testing the air, snarling then Dean advanced straight at them. He fired off another errant shot, and then another, and the echoes mounted furiously into a dry thunder, and the air stank with barrel smoke. Anna came up out of that sandy crater and was right by Dean pouring light into their numbers, flaring it, spotting it.

There was already confusion and panic amidst those sidling paws and lit-upon eyes, when Dean suddenly rushed them like some fiend out of an ancient curse, howling with that raw voice of his until it broke down mercilessly, and firing off shot after shot as their ranks broke and they ran yammering for the hills.

By the time their footfalls were gone beyond the rim of those smoky barrens, Dean had collapsed down upon his knees.

⁓

ANNA TOOK HOLD and steadied him. They then began the half-mile march into the torched hills, wearing goggles and breathing masks, for the wind had picked up and so had resurrected more fire. They looked like alien creatures moving through an otherworldly landscape.

Finally, they stood at the edge of the culvert where Dean's body had been borne beyond the limits of endurance. Anna took off her mask. She had the cloth strip from the pillow, and she smelled it and put it away and began to walk about trying to pick up Giv's scent.

Dean took from the carryall the bullhorn. He removed his mask and with that graveled voice called out, "Giv!"

He listened through the echo to the silence and he watched, but there was only a dull wind driving sand over that ravaged hide of an earth.

When Dean turned, he found Anna had walked a ways up the hill. He called to her, "Not . . ." he pointed downslope, ". . . this way?"

She said no.

When Dean got alongside Anna, she said, "There's something."

"Giv?"

She did not answer. She did not want to confess what she'd picked up was a scent of death. She pointed across the culvert, so that was where they went.

The terrain was bald rock and challenging drops. Through his mask, Dean asked again about the scent she had picked up, and yet again she did not answer. Where they had crossed the culvert was a crack, and escaping water eroded a slight crevasse that was still wet and went on for yards through a crooked decline with meandering gaps strung together by time and circumstance. Anna followed it till she was stopped by what she saw.

He lay there in death. Torn from throat to shoulder by bared teeth. And as the sound of chopper blades swept down the culvert, she knelt over the killed wolf. Dean hovered behind her, and had it not been for the goggles and breathing mask and layers of western dust, he might have read the dread and anticipation expressed on her features.

Anna stood. "He's close."

Dean pressed ahead down a rutted path where the ground was littered with paw tracks that spoke to a world of fighting and chaos.

The path led them a little farther on to an inscription of rock. They entered this cul-de-sac, side by side, over ground that had been fought for with blood, and in that lonely place, shaped by centuries, was a hollow tombface in the stone where the water trail went.

Dean called out, "Giv?" Anna bent down to try and see, and as the dust cleared around that stony entrance a muzzle and a pair of eyes appeared.

In a sort of wonder, Anna ran to the entrance and now Dean saw too. Giv . . . Perro Grande . . . was dragging himself from the dark reaches to open arms.

He lay in Dean's lap exhausted and bloody, having survived on tricklets of water, but his tail told it all and the affection in the way he licked Dean's face. And when he smelled Anna's hand—a world lost to him had been returned. From the deepest reaches of his existence, his whole body came alive. He tried to stand as he could not contain all he felt.

They had to make him lie still, so they could splint his leg. Then Anna injected him to cut the pain and get him quiescent. He could rest and be weary, for he was safe now, in the security of those who loved him.

They had been spotted and word spread as word will, and soon news choppers rushed the scene. Search-and-Rescue sent down a harness for the dog.

The choppers hovered tentatively upon the thermals until finally, through waves of grey, Giv ascended.

He was, at first, this apparition against the long light over the rimland—there, then gone in the smoke, the cable that bore him impossible to see.

And so Giv rose until he was above the smoke and upon a shoreless sky. He was, thought Dean, bearing all their stories now. From St. Peter's to a most precious act of sacrifice.

And of that pawn ticket—it would prove to have its place and meaning. It turned out the shop existed in East St. Louis, Illinois. The ticket was for a trunk. And when that trunk arrived at St. Peter's, Anna discovered among its contents a history of Giv's father, and the story of his people, and the America that shaped those days. But that is for another book, at another time. The pages here that I, Dean Hickok, Sergeant, late of the U.S. Marines, was compelled to write, are for now, and for you.

⁓

THERE ARE ENDLESS legends about dogs. Countless books telling of their kind in myth. No culture is complete without them.

There is one that might have special relevance. It says that when God was about the creation he cleaved the earth. On one side of this expanding abyss was man, on the other all the rest of God's living creations. But, as the breach widened, the dog leapt that channel to join man.

It was in that moment, through that act, the dog proved to be everything that God had in mind for the creation known as man. The dog had leapt the channel, for the dog loved man and wanted kinship with man. He wanted his goodness to walk side by side with man's.

It was also an act of rebellion. This, too, proved to be part of everything God had in mind for man. Rebellion has its place. It is a gift, as wisdom can be a gift, as prudence, or charity. It is essential to the essence of God's creation— the power to choose freely who one will or will not be. And will one be worthy of the living creature that leapt the abyss?